Mildred Cabell Watkins

American Literature

Mildred Cabell Watkins

American Literature

ISBN/EAN: 9783743331730

Manufactured in Europe, USA, Canada, Australia, Japa

Cover: Foto ©Andreas Hilbeck / pixelio.de

Manufactured and distributed by brebook publishing software
(www.brebook.com)

Mildred Cabell Watkins

American Literature

AMERICAN
LITERATURE

BY

MILDRED CABELL WATKINS

NEW YORK ·:· CINCINNATI ·:· CHICAGO

AMERICAN BOOK COMPANY

PREFACE.

In this volume the story of American literature is briefly told for the benefit of young Americans. It is written in a style which is both simple and familiar, avoiding on the one hand the verbiage of the larger manuals for schools, and on the other the prattle of the so-called first books for children. Brevity rather than condensation has been sought; care has been taken not to encumber the text with unnecessary or irrelevant details; dates have in most cases been relegated to the summaries at the close of the various chapters; criticisms are brief, often summed up in a single terse, easily remembered expression; illustrative extracts are confined to familiar quotations with which everybody ought to be acquainted. In the preparation of the book four objects have been constantly borne in mind: (1) to make the study interesting; (2) to give due prominence to the most essential facts; (3) to lead students to a first-hand acquaintance with the best and most famous works of American authors; and (4) to meet a very general demand among teachers for a simple, practical text book on the history of our literature adapted to the comprehension of pupils in the elementary schools.

A good deal of space has necessarily been given to minor authors and to living writers who will probably be forgotten before another century. But although these play only an insignificant part in the real history of our literature, it is nevertheless important that readers should learn something about the writers whose books are affording so much present enjoyment to the world. On the other hand many names have been omitted—names known to the readers of news-stand literature, some of them very popular, but all of short-lived notoriety. This omission is defensible on the ground that some of the most widely read books of the day have no more place in literature than has the popular newspaper or last year's almanac.

In placing this little work before the public it is confidently hoped that it will encourage its readers—and especially its younger readers—to become more intimately acquainted with the works of the best American authors. It is also hoped that, by making the study of the subject both easy and attractive, the task of teachers and of others intrusted with the duty of forming and guiding the literary tastes of young people will be somewhat lightened.

CONTENTS:

AMERICAN LITERATURE.

CHAPTER I.

What does "American Literature" Mean? — If we should accept the definition sometimes given for literature, and say that it is "all that has been written," then "American literature" would, of course, include everything written by Americans, and the longest life would not be long enough to master its study. But the expression has generally a more restricted meaning, and includes, not all that has been written, but only what was worth writing and worth reading — worth reading not only when first printed, but for years afterwards. Sometimes, it is true, it includes books which nobody reads to-day, but which were written by men who influenced their own times, molding people's thoughts and actions, and thus shaping the literature of our own day, just as childhood shapes the after life of the man.

The study of American literature, then, is the study of the best books of America, and also of the lives of the men and women who wrote them. Volumes like the present try to answer the question: "What Americans have written books worth reading?" They try to tell, too, where and when such authors lived, what they wrote, how they wrote; sometimes why they wrote; and, in general, what kind of persons they were. So small a volume as this can tell you little, very little; but it is hoped that it will make you wish to learn more and will make you read what the men and women mentioned in it have written. American literature is only a branch which has shot forth from the great tree of English literature, shot forth vigorously and independently in this century; for our ancestors coming from England brought with them English books, and it was long before they felt the need of any of their own production.

Great Names in our Literature.—You need not expect to find many *great* names among our writers, for only two or three geniuses appear in a century, and our literature is only a hundred years old, which is very young for a national literature. We have never produced a Shakespeare or a Milton. Few have brought a new message that they *must* tell, yet very many have told the old truths and messages in a very charming way, and often in a new way. There are hundreds who instruct and entertain us— so many, indeed, that it is hard to make a selection. Not more than the names can be mentioned of some, especially of those living now. Their books are the *read* books of to-day; but it will take until the twentieth century to know whether they have any right to be considered *great* books.

Periods of Growth. — Our literature had its very feeble beginning in the *Colonial Period*, 1607–1765. It gave some indications of improvement and growth during the *Revolutionary Period*, 1765–1800. But it was scarcely worthy of the name until the beginning of the *National Period*, or nineteenth century. This period may, for convenience, be divided into the years *before the war* and the years *after the war*.

CHAPTER II.

The First American Book.—In 1607 the first permanent English colony was planted at Jamestown, Virginia, and in 1608 the first book written by an English colonist about America was printed in England. It was by John Smith, of whom you have read such romantic stories in your school history, and for the sake of brevity it may be called *A True Account of Virginia*. The whole name is five lines long, for it was usual then to make the titles of books a summary of their contents. Generally these titles are about all that one needs to know nowadays of the whole volume. John Smith wrote eight other books about America, and several other Virginia colonists kept chronicles of the events happening in the settlement. It is thought that Shakespeare[1] may have read one of these old chronicles, and that a certain shipwreck described in it suggested the incidents in *The Tempest*, a play of his; for Shakespeare was alive when Jamestown was built.

Dependence upon England.—None of these annals were printed in Virginia, for she had no printing press. Neither had she schools; the wealthy men sent their sons back to England to be educated, for

---

[1] William Shakespeare (1564–1616), an English dramatist, or writer of plays for the theater, and one of the greatest of all writers.

they still regarded England as "home." They were Englishmen living in Virginia, trying to procure from field and forest a better support than they could find in their own land. Fighting famine and Indians, felling forests, founding homes modeled as far as possible after those which they had left, were labors which left little time and thought for writing. Only their letters to friends in England and a few rude chronicles give any account of the new world which they were exploring, and in which they were beginning to lay the foundations of a new empire.

The Puritans. — A very different class of people laid the beginnings of New England. The Puritans, who came over in the "Mayflower" in 1620, were searching for a spot where they and their children might have the right to worship God according to the dictates of their conscience. Hardly had their rough log cabins been built as shelters for their wives and little ones before a church and a schoolhouse were erected in each settlement. Not willing to be dependent on England for the education of their sons, they founded in 1636 Harvard College, "intended to train men for the ministry," and there more of our writers have been educated than at any other college.

Religious Controversies. — Though the Puritans, too, were very busy fighting Indians and founding homes and villages, they took time to fight each other on religious questions, and their bitter disputes filled many volumes. The Revs. Thomas Hooker, John Cotton, and Roger Williams were among the most voluminous of these writers. Nobody reads their works now, and we remember and love only one of the three, Roger Williams. The other religious disputants were good men and learned men; their sermons and many theological writings were highly prized by the Puritans, and had great influ-

ence. But tastes and beliefs have undergone a great
change since then. We are shocked at the way in
which Quakers and all "unorthodox" people were
persecuted — everybody that did not believe exactly
as the Puritans believed being called "unorthodox."
Roger Williams thought as we do about this persecution, and was himself driven out of Massachusetts
for his religious views.

John Eliot. — One name belonging to the seventeenth century deserves to be mentioned with those
of the heroes of the Scriptures — that of the Rev.
John Eliot, or the "apostle to the Indians." Going
out among the savages as a teacher, he patiently set
himself to the task of translating the Bible into their
language — a mighty undertaking; for the Indians
having no written speech, he had to create one for
them. It was the first Bible printed in America.
To his last breath Eliot labored among the Indians,
and on the very day of his death the feeble old man
was found teaching the alphabet to an Indian lad
who sat by his bedside. Eliot also helped to compile the first book printed in our country, the *Bay
Psalm Book*, which appeared in 1640, the first printing press in our country having been set up the year
previous at Cambridge, Massachusetts.

Early Attempts at Poetry. — The *Bay Psalm
Book* sets the psalms in miserable verse; but it was
used even in England in the churches, though we
are utterly unable to comprehend how anybody could
sing such poor stuff. Nor can we understand how
the Puritans could admire the dreary lines of Mrs.
Anne Bradstreet, whom they thought a poet. Poetry
was not in their line. Only two among them —
Mrs. Bradstreet and Michael Wigglesworth — even
attempted to cultivate it.

Histories. — Several of the colonists attempted to

write " histories," for they appreciated the fact that they were building what was to be a great nation, and amid their stern and stirring occupations they tried to record the happenings in the colony.   William Bradford and John Winthrop were two who published these quaint daily jottings or diaries.   These ancient records are intensely dry, tedious reading, and yet some of our loveliest poems and stories have been woven out of the materials found in them.

The Mathers. — One remarkable family lived through the seventeenth century and into the eighteenth — the Mathers, all preachers and all leading men, whose words and opinions had great weight. Rev. Increase Mather, the author of a hundred books, collected, under the name of *Illustrious Providences*, marvelous ghost stories and strange tales of mysterious events.   He was the sixth president of Harvard College.   His son, Cotton Mather, must have diligently read this collection, for he had much to do with the Salem witchcraft affair, and approved mightily of torturing, burning, and hanging the poor creatures who were accused of being witches.   He was an extraordinary man.   At eleven he entered Harvard College, at fifteen he was a graduate, and afterwards a preacher.   Yet in the midst of other duties he published about four hundred books, counting pamphlets and all !   No wonder he had the largest library then in America — his own volumes alone were sufficient to furnish a good start.   His chief work, *Magnalia*, was more generally read than any other book of that place and period.   It is a curious mixture, and is intended to be an ecclesiastical or church history of New England, or, as the author puts it, an account of " the great things done by Christ for the American people."   The name is much more attractive than the interior.

Other Writers.—Other colleges—William and Mary in Virginia, and Yale (1700) in Connecticut—were founded. Authors increased, and quite a list could be made from both Virginia and New England. Some of their works are found even now on library shelves, but they would hardly interest young folks. The *New England Primer*, in which our little ancestors learned their letters, is an amusing curiosity. A few of its pages are the most popular of anything that has survived of Rev. John Cotton—for 'twas he who got it up. Here is a specimen of the a-b-c's:

> "A.   In Adam's fall
> We sinned all.
>
> Z.   Zaccheus he
> Did climb a tree
> Our Lord to see."

Summary.[1]—SEVENTEENTH CENTURY.

Annalists: William Bradford and John Winthrop, both born in 1588, and both governors of one of the colonies. *History of Plymouth Plantation*, by the former; *History of New England*, by the latter.

Theological writers: Revs. Thomas Hooker, John Cotton, and Roger Williams.

Rev. John Eliot (1604–90), "apostle to the Indians," translated the Bible into the Indian dialect, and helped compile *Bay Psalm Book*.

Rev. Increase Mather, author of a hundred books. His son, Rev. Cotton Mather (1663–1728), author of about four hundred books, the most important being *Magnalia*.

Poets (?): Mrs. Anne Bradstreet (1612–72), Michael Wigglesworth (1631–1715).

---

[1] The summaries are not intended to be studied by the pupils as exercises of memory; they are only for reference.

CHAPTER III.

JONATHAN EDWARDS, THINKER AND THEOLOGIAN.

Two Great Men. — In the last chapter you read of men whose names are almost forgotten, whose books, found only in a few special collections, are never disturbed by any reader except by historians or those who make it their delight to search into old, dusty records of the past; but there are two men of Colonial times whose memory will never die, and whose views and sayings are still quoted and have an important influence. One of them, Benjamin Franklin, belongs partly to the Revolutionary period; the other, Jonathan Edwards, died several years before the Revolution.

Boyhood of Jonathan Edwards. — From his very babyhood Jonathan Edwards showed signs of having an unusual mind and disposition. His heart was full of religious thoughts, of reachings out towards God. A diary which he kept astonishes us by its solemn words, — for it gives his inner feelings, — and his acts are just like his words. Children were rarely permitted to join the church in those days; but he was a very tiny lad when he became a member, and even then he had fixed on the rules which should guide his life, rules which he afterwards wrote out in seventy resolutions, and faithfully kept. Even when a boy he used to call together his schoolmates and hold prayer meetings, and it was his habit to go off from others five times a day that he might pray. On leaving college he dedicated himself to God, "never to be in any respect his own."

His mind developed early, like his soul; he loved to think on deep questions, to look inside his mind to see its workings. A book called Locke's [1] *Essay on the Human Understanding* came in his way, and it was like stumbling on a discovery of gold and silver. It probably shaped his life; for he became, like Locke, one of the world's greatest mental philosophers. He was also one of her grandest preachers. "The first man of the world of the eighteenth century in its first quarter," "The grandest theologian since St. Paul," he has been called. Even those who do not believe his doctrines at all acknowledge that he was a wonderful reasoner and thinker, and a holy man in daily life, full of love, faith, and good works. Yet this distinguished person lived the life of a hard-working village and country preacher, dying at fifty-five, just when his fellow-countrymen and the church, having waked up to his genius, had called him to a higher position.

Born in East Windsor, Connecticut, in 1703, entering Yale at thirteen, being graduated at seventeen, he was at nineteen a pastor in New York City. For two years he was tutor at Yale; but his heart was in the pulpit, and he accepted the pastorate of Northampton, Massachusetts, where he remained twenty-four years, doing great good, and rising to the highest place among the preachers and learned men of the land. His people, however, complained of his preaching as too plain and severe, and he was forced to leave Northampton. He next went out as a missionary among the Indians of western Massachusetts, living at Stockbridge; and there, with his wife and ten

1 John Locke (1632-1704), a great mental philosopher of England, who first studied and described the mind.

children to support, pressed by poverty, overwhelmed with work, he stayed for eight years. Though preaching four times a day, twice in English and twice in Indian, besides catechising — though studying " until there was scarcely any branch of knowledge he was not master of," it was here he wrote his most famous work, *The Freedom of the Will*, the deepest and most original in theological and metaphysical thought. He wrote also a *Life of David Brainerd*, a missionary to the Indians, and a volume entitled *The Religious Affections.*

Theological thought is thought about God and religious opinions; metaphysical thought is thought about the mind itself, our wills, our motives, etc. *The Freedom of the Will* includes both, and is on a question which theologians have been discussing for more than a thousand years. This question is: " How far can people choose for themselves, and how far does God govern their wills and choice ?" It was a difficult question, and Edwards tried to explain the difficulty by saying that we are responsible for any evil we do, yet we can't have even one good thought unless God gives it to us. It is as good an explanation, perhaps, as can be made of what nobody can understand or need understand; and it has been praised and abused as most other deep doctrines of theology have been. It was a most remarkable volume to be written by a poor missionary, and in six months' time — so remarkable that its author was asked to become president of the College of New Jersey (Princeton). In less than five weeks after he took the place he died of smallpox, but not before the title " President Edwards " had been fastened on him.

His sermons were as powerful as his books, and had much influence. He came when the church was indifferent, and he preached reform, telling of

sin and punishment so much that his religion seems
more gloomy than ours of to-day.   He was brought
up a strict Puritan ; but however hard his words and
beliefs seem, he himself was humble and lovely in
heart and conduct.   His writings only theologians
read ; not much of them would be comprehended by
young people ; but they still have a place of honor on
the bookshelves of theological students.

Summary. — JONATHAN EDWARDS (1703–58), theologian, metaphysician, and preacher.   Born in
  Connecticut; preached at Northampton and
  Stockbridge, Massachusetts ; was made president
  of Princeton College in 1758. Books : *The Freedom of the Will, The Religious Affections,* and *Life
  of David Brainerd.*

First Five of the Seventy Resolutions of Jonathan Edwards.

  1. Resolved, That I will do whatever I think most to
the glory of God and my own good, profit, and pleasure
in the *whole* of my duration, without any consideration of
the time, whether now, or never so many myriads of ages
hence.
  2. Resolved, To do whatever I think to be my duty and
most for the good of mankind in general.
  3. Resolved, Never to lose one moment of time, but to
improve it in the most profitable way I possibly can.
  4. Resolved, To live with all my might while I do live.
  5. Resolved, Never to do anything which I should be
afraid to do if it were the last hour of my life.

Definition of Religion.

  True religion in a great measure consists in holy affections.   A love of divine things for the beauty and sweetness of their moral excellency is the spring of all holy
affections.

CHAPTER IV.

BENJAMIN FRANKLIN, THE PRACTICAL THINKER.

Boyhood of Franklin.—While little Jonathan Edwards was being carefully trained in the family circle and schoolroom and was learning about God, the Bible, and spiritual things, another little boy was training himself, and was learning all about the people and the world around him. For as one was to be the deepest of thinkers, the other was to be the most active of thinkers. The name of this boy was Benjamin Franklin. As he *did* far more than he *wrote*, his place is rather in history than in literature, and living nearly through the eighteenth century he belongs to both the Colonial and the Revolutionary periods. He was born in Boston in 1706, in a home full of children, but lacking money, for his father was a tallow-chandler, or candle-maker. He went to school only two years, being taken away when he was ten that he might help with the candle-making. The little fellow loved books as much as Jonathan Edwards loved them; but the library to which the minister's son had access was very different from the bookshelf in the shop. Besides theological discussions, which young Franklin detested, there were three works that influenced him. These were *Plutarch's* [1] *Lives*, an *Essay on Projects*, and es-

---

[1] Plutarch, ancient biographer, wrote *Lives* of famous Greeks and Romans.

pecially Cotton Mather's *Essays to Do Good.* Certainly Franklin's chief occupations in manhood were trying new projects — nearly always successful ones — and doing good for his country and for mankind. During the two years in his father's shop, by using his bright eyes, quick ears, and active mind, he had educated himself so well that he was put as an apprentice in his brother's printing office.

He Learns Printing. — He was glad of the change because of the chance it gave him to read more books ; for he had read all he could get, and spent all of his little money for more. His first collection was John Bunyan's [1] works, *Pilgrim's Progress* having pleased him ; but he soon exchanged these for some historical works. It took him only four years to learn thoroughly the art of printing, but being unable to endure his brother's unkind treatment he ran off to Philadelphia. This was the time he bought the bread and went up the street holding one roll under each arm and eating another. You remember how a young girl, afterwards his wife, stood in her door and laughed at him. He got employment in a printing office in Philadelphia, and was afterwards in England for a year engaged in the same trade. Fortunately for America, he returned to this country, and after a while was able to start his own newspaper, in Philadelphia.

Poor Richard's Almanac. — He also issued *Poor Richard's Almanac*, a yearly publication full of shrewd, sharp sayings about carefulness, industry, and economy. Almanacs were very important publications then. More than half the non-religious books printed during Franklin's boyhood were almanacs. In many

---

[1] John Bunyan, a Baptist preacher of the seventeenth century, once an ignorant tinker, was the author of the best allegory ever written, *Pilgrim's Progress.*

houses an almanac and a Bible were the only books. The former was consulted about earthly matters as the latter about heavenly matters; for its pages gave information about the weather, the crops, etc., and on its margins were jotted all the important events in the family, and all business accounts. *Poor Richard's Almanac* was so much the best that it soon took the place of all others, and its wise maxims were in people's mouths nearly as often as Bible verses. Indeed, I have heard people quote Franklin's proverbs as Solomon's, though they are generally very different. These homely sayings had a wonderful effect on the New England colonists: they helped to make them sharp, business-like, active, cautious, hard-working, saving. Franklin was the first well-known type and the best type of the true " Yankee."   .

What Franklin wrote was a tiny fraction of what he did. He had no ambition to be a writer, and what he did publish was dashed off carelessly while he was performing the work of ten or twenty ordinary men. Two old volumes, large ones, lie before me, and the title-page, *Memoirs of Benjamin Franklin, written by Himself;* . . . *with his Social Epistolary Correspondence, Philosophical, Political, and Moral Letters and Essays*, gives us an idea of the nature of what he wrote. The *Memoirs*, or autobiography, is still often read. His *Poor Richard's Almanac* does not need to be read, for a large part of it is known by heart, having passed from mouth to mouth. The philosophical and political papers are on questions of that day, and are of little interest now. He was an enthusiastic natural philosopher: when he proved by his experiment with a kite and key — you have heard of it often — that lightning is electricity, he says he was happy enough to die.

His Public Services. — But it was in Revolutionary times that Franklin became one of the founders of the United States. His name is signed to both the Declaration of Independence and the Constitution. Having been sent as ambassador to France, he gained that treaty for us which probably saved our country. He organized our postal system, traveling with his daughter Sallie in his private gig all through the thirteen colonies to do it. The American Philosophical Society and the University of Pennsylvania were founded by him, and the first public library and the first hospital were the results of his suggestions. Yet amid all his heavy cares he took thought for smaller improvements, giving Philadelphia a police, a fire, and a street-cleaning department, and inventing lightning rods and the Franklin stove. No man was better known, more honored, more consulted. Europe showered distinctions on him. Oxford University, England's famous college, as well as our colleges, made him "Dr." Franklin. Nor did success and popularity spoil him. He continued to practice simplicity and frugality. If he had devoted his days to literature what could he not have left to the world? But his unlimited "common sense" was needed by his country, his State, and his city, and except in his letters, which are models, we can form little idea of the greatness of the man from his writings.

Summary. — DR. BENJAMIN FRANKLIN (1706–90). Boston his birthplace, Philadelphia his home in manhood. Few advantages; son of a candlemaker; apprenticed to his brother, learns printing as a trade. Prominent as a natural philosopher, but more especially as a statesman and the establisher of practical reforms. Works: *Autobiography, Poor Richard's Almanac*, many papers on political, scientific, and moral questions, and letters.   Not so much a writer as a doer, belonging more to history than to literature.

Some of Franklin's Sayings: from Father Abraham's Speech (1757).

(After Franklin had published *Poor Richard's Almanac* for twenty-five years, he " formed " the proverbs, " which contained the wisdom of many ages and nations, into a connected discourse," thus collecting the scattered sayings ; and he puts the discourse into the mouth of a " wise old man " talking to people who had come to an auction.   This speech was copied, Franklin's *Autobiography* tells us, " in all the newspapers of the American continent ; reprinted in Britain on a large sheet of paper to be stuck up in houses ; two translations were made of it in France, and great numbers bought by the clergy and gentry to distribute gratis among their poor parishioners and tenants.   In Pennsylvania some thought it had its share of influence in producing that growing plenty of money observable for several years after its publication.")

God helps them that help themselves.
But dost thou love life, then do not squander time, for that is the stuff life is made of.
What we call time enough always proves little enough.
There are no gains without pains.
He that hath a trade hath an estate.
Diligence is the mother of good luck.
One to-day is worth two to-morrows.
Never leave that till to-morrow which you can do to-day.
Little strokes fell large oaks.
For want of a nail the shoe was lost, and for want of a shoe the horse was lost, and for want of a horse the rider was lost, being overtaken and slain by the enemy ; all for want of a little care about a horseshoe nail.
It is foolish to lay out money in a purchase of repentance.
Experience keeps a dear school, but fools will learn in no other.

CHAPTER V.

Orators and Statesmen. — From 1765 until the early part of the present century two great questions were in the minds of the American people: up to the close of the Revolution it was the separation from England; after the Revolution it was the formation of a government for the separated country. Hence great speeches or political papers came from the brains and pens of those capable of making a literature. Such men cared not for fame as writers, — they wrote for the particular crisis which they were passing through, — and their works are not read much to-day. The school readers which our grandfathers used were composed almost entirely of these speeches. School-boys still go to them for declamations, and political leaders draw upon them for their editorials and their discussions. The times called for great men, and great men rose to meet the call. They belong to history, for they are Patrick Henry, Jefferson, Adams, Hamilton, and other orators and statesmen. "Give me liberty or give me death" has been recited in every school-house, and has awakened in boys an enthusiasm for freedom, as it did in the General Assembly in Virginia. One sentence from a statesman of the eighteenth century, Josiah Quincy, describes the feelings of that day: "To hope for the protection of Heaven without doing our duty and exerting ourselves as becomes men, is to mock the Deity. However righteous our

23

cause, we cannot at this period of the world expect a miraculous salvation. Heaven will undoubtedly assist us if we act like men." Another sentence, " These are the times that try men's souls," describes those fiery days, being the first words of the *Crisis*, a periodical issued occasionally by Thomas Paine. The first number of the *Crisis* came out in 1776, and was, by the order of Washington, read to all the American troops. Paine, though born in England, was very earnest on the side of the colonists, and helped the cause by his pamphlet entitled *Common Sense*. *The Rights of Man* was more read and better liked in France and England than any other political paper published at that time. His *Age of Reason* was an attack on the Bible, which did some harm then, but which is now regarded as feeble and coarse, and is without influence.

Political Parties.—After the American people were free from England a Constitution was drawn up. After it was drawn up some approved of it, some did not. Some wished the government to have a great deal of power, some wished the States to keep much freedom. Two parties accordingly arose, the Federalists and the Anti-Federalists, and there was much writing on both sides, many pamphlets pouring forth. The strongest pieces appeared in the *Federalist*, a series of papers on political subjects. Alexander Hamilton wrote more than half of these.

Thomas Jefferson was the originator of what was then called the Republican-Democratic party which most of the Anti-Federalists joined. It was he who drew up the Declaration of Independence. He was very learned in the principles of government. His autobiography and state and political papers are his literary remains; he wrote also *Notes on Virginia*.

Madison and States' Rights.—Another early

President, James Madison, is sometimes called the father of the Constitution, he had so much to do with shaping it.   He was the promoter of the famous " States' rights " doctrine, that the States, having united of their own accord to make the United States, had a right to leave the Union if the federal government did not perform its part of the compact.   This was the doctrine of the South when it seceded in 1861.   Madison and Chief-Justice Jay wrote the other papers of the *Federalist.*

Poetry. — Even the poets wrote political poems calling to Liberty and ridiculing the Tories.   The most influential in sending the volunteers laughing into Washington's army was Judge John Trumbull with his witty poem entitled *McFingal.*   It describes a wordy quarrel between the Whigs and Tories, — those for and those against the Revolution, — the quarrel ending in " a free fight around a liberty-pole."   Several of the lines are still quoted.   Another piece intended to make the British appear absurd is *The Battle of the Kegs*, by Francis Hopkinson.   His son Joseph wrote *Hail Columbia, Happy Land*, our national ode.   This recalls *Columbia, Columbia, to Glory Arise*, by Timothy Dwight, grandson of Jonathan Edwards.   As a theologian and president of Yale College he was a man of importance then, but his volume of poetry is very dull.   We all have heard his version of the 137th Psalm, *I Love Thy Kingdom, Lord.*   Philip Freneau, a popular political and humorous poet, was the most graceful of any who tried to make verses, as his more sentimental lines on *The Wild Honeysuckle* and his *Indian Burying-ground* show.   Freneau was a strong Anti-Federalist.   Joel Barlow tried to be a poet, and succeeded in thinking himself one, but nobody else agrees with him.   His attempt to make a great American epic, telling the history of the nation, was a miserable failure. His *Hasty Pudding* is amusing, but the *Columbiad* has nothing to recommend it. He was an active politician.

Biographies. — Chief-Justice Marshall's *Life of Washington* and William Wirt's *Life of Patrick Henry* are not entirely forgotten biographies written by Virginians as well as of Virginians. Wirt wrote also a description of Virginia, and the school readers used to contain a favorite piece by him. It is an account of Virginia's blind preacher Waddell, and is from his *Letters of a British Spy.*

The First Novelist. — None of these men, however, made a profession of literature. They wrote in order to accomplish some object, or in some moment less busy than usual they sent forth a poem. One man only, Charles Brockden Brown, did try to make his life one devoted to literature. Several novels, wild stories and very gloomy, appeared by him before 1800, and he tried his hand at essays, political pieces, geographies, histories, almost everything. He attempted to found literary magazines. But the new country was not ready for a literature of its own : the inhabitants were too few, and the readers still fewer. One of Brown's novels, *Arthur Mervyn*, describes vividly the yellow-fever epidemic that came upon Philadelphia in 1793. Brown, always very delicate in health, died too early to see his country take the place he longed for it to take in literature.

Summary of Revolutionary Period. — Chiefly orators and statesmen. The *Federalist* contained the finest political papers.

Leading Statesmen : Alexander Hamilton (1757–1804). Thomas Jefferson (1743–1826), Virginia ; besides Declaration of Independence and political papers, *Notes on Virginia* and *Memoirs* of his own life.   James Madison (1751–1836).   John Adams (1735–1826).   Chief-Justice Jay (1745–1829) wrote for the *Federalist*.   Two orators: Josiah Quincy (1744–75), Patrick Henry (1736–99). Chief-Justice Marshall (1755–1835), Virginia, statesman and author of *Life of Washington*. William Wirt (1772–1834), Virginia, orator ; *Life of Patrick Henry; Letters of a British Spy.* Thomas Paine (1737–1809), England ; by his paper the *Crisis*, and by his *Common Sense*, aided the cause of independence ; *The Rights of Man; Age of Reason*, an infidel work.

Poets: John Trumbull (1750–1831), *McFingal*, a burlesque.   Francis Hopkinson (1737–91), *Battle of the Kegs.*   Joseph Hopkinson (1770–1842), *Hail Columbia.*   Timothy Dwight (1752–1817), *Columbia, Columbia, to Glory Arise*, and the hymn, *I Love Thy Kingdom, Lord.*   Joel Barlow (1754–1812), *Columbiad*, very poor ; *Hasty Pudding.*   Philip Freneau (1752–1832), political and humorous poems very popular in *his* day ; remembered by the more sentimental *Lines to a Wild Honeysuckle* and *The Indian Burying-ground.*

First Novelist: Charles Brockden Brown (1771–1810), first to make a profession of literature, wrote several romances : *Arthur Mervyn, Wieland*, etc.

CHAPTER VI.

Childhood and Youth. — In the City of New York, April 3, 1783, a father and a mother were looking at a tiny babe and discussing what its name should be. "General Washington's work is done," said the mother; "let us name our boy after him;" for she had a fond mother's hope that her son might take the place and perform the work left by such men as Washington. Once only did General Washington see this namesake: he came into a store where the Scotch nurse was standing, and she eagerly held out the little fellow, saying, "This bairn is named after you;" whereupon a hand was laid upon the "bairn's" head and a kindly blessing bestowed — a great event in the family. This laddie was Washington Irving, who was afterwards called the father of our literature, as Washington himself is called the father of our country. He was the first American recognized in Europe as a writer; the first almost who had no political or religious views to teach, but tried only to entertain and instruct his readers. Earlier writers cared only for *what* they said: Irving cared *how* he said it; therefore he wrote in a clear, beautiful style or manner. Yet he did not for a long time show how talented he was; for it was hard for him to learn his letters, and he disliked to study. He loved to read, however, and did not object to writing compositions, for he was willing to write compositions in exchange for having his examples in arithmetic worked. Puritan days and ideas were not over, and Mr. Irving, a Scotch Presbyterian, was strict with his family, not approving of many amusements and much pleasure ; and sometimes Washington slipped away at night to amusements, though he never dared to miss family prayers. Mrs. Irving was a sweet, gentle English lady, not so strict as her husband, especially with Washington, the baby of the household. All his ten brothers and sisters seem to have spoiled him, partly because he was the youngest, partly because he was delicate, and partly, I think, because of his sweet, sunny disposition. Owing to his delicate health he was not made to study, and on leaving school he spent much of his time wandering round the country with his dog and his gun. Years afterwards he showed that the wanderings had not been vacant, idle wanderings; for he described all that region so charmingly, and told such quaint legends of hill and brook, that we know he was seeing, listening, thinking, as he tramped about seeking health and hunting game. Another favorite amusement that he turned into use when a writer was wandering into the Dutch part of the city. New York was then a town of not more than twenty-five thousand inhabitants, and was part Dutch and part English, the two peoples having very little to do with each other. The lad delighted to listen to the legends which the Dutch told of the very country he had hunted in ; he remembered these legends, and with many changes retold them in his books. He noticed, too, every oddity of his Dutch acquaintances ; for he was full of quiet fun, and enjoyed the smiling side of everything.

Law and Love. — When sixteen years of age he was put into the office of Josiah O. Hoffmann to

study law; but he learned more love than law, for
Mr. Hoffmann had a sweet young daughter, Matilda,
and she was soon engaged to the attractive law student, who read poetry with so much expression and
knew about nearly every book except his law books.
Her death at eighteen was a lasting grief to Irving,
for his attachment to her was one of the deepest feelings of his nature, so deep that he never married.

His Tour Abroad. — His sorrow may have injured
his health, as in 1804, or when he was twenty-one,
his family became very much alarmed about his
condition, and to save his life sent him on a voyage
to Europe.   He was so white and thin, so racked by
his cough, that many of his friends had no hope of
ever seeing him again; but he spent a delightful two
years traveling through England, Holland, France,
Switzerland, and Italy, returning home much more
vigorous than ever before.   While abroad he had
made up his mind to be a painter, but after trying
three days gave it up.   When he came back to New
York he was admitted to the bar as a lawyer, the only
profession he had any knowledge of, and this knowledge was, as we have seen, neither deep nor full.
He never pleaded a case, and was a lawyer only in
name, not in practice.

Up to this time no American had succeeded in
making writing a profession — only one had tried to
do it, even.   There were no large publishing houses
then, no wealthy men fond of books and willing to
help a young author.   The few States then forming
the United States did not have many more people than
the State of New York contains to-day, and these few
seemed to be well content with their small stock of
English books.   Settling new States left little leisure
for reading.   Consequently Washington Irving does
not seem to have thought of supporting himself by his

pen. All he had written so far was a series of letters in a local paper, letters in a satirical or half-mocking vein, which were signed " Jonathan Oldstyle." Thus he drifted on, indulged by his older brothers, who allowed him to be the society gentleman of the family, much to the pleasure of society. So sweet and cheery-tempered was he that he could not fail to be popular, especially with educated men, as he had read so extensively. Yet he was ashamed of doing nothing, and endeavored to learn enough commercial arithmetic to help his brothers in their business. But the boy who did not work his examples at school had no talent as an accountant. He deserves credit for trying in spite of his dislike for such study.

"**Salmagundi.**"—Wearying of commercial arithmetic, he joined with his brother William and a friend, James K. Paulding, in bringing out a periodical called *Salmagundi*, an Italian name signifying "a mixture" or "a hash." William Irving furnished the poetry, the other two the prose, which consisted of essays, tales, etc., somewhat like the papers in the *Spectator.*[1] The object of the paper was the same as that of the *Spectator*, "to reform the town." The publishers became tired of their venture before their subscribers did, and only twenty numbers were issued. The political pieces were full of humor, but were not in support of any party.

"**Knickerbocker's History of New York.**"— A bright idea had meanwhile crept into Irving's brain, and this was to write a burlesque or mock history of New York, describing its manners and customs when it was still New Amsterdam and settled by the Dutch. When a boy his observation had made men-

---

[1] The *Spectator*, one of the first periodicals of England, begun in 1711, issued daily, and having great literary influence in its day. Joseph Addison wrote the greater part of it.

tal photographs of the Dutch part of the city: his
memory had kept the pictures unfaded, his fancy and
imagination had painted and enlarged these pictures.
Arranged together they made one of the funniest volumes ever written. Representing himself as Diedrich Knickerbocker, a Dutchman, he called the book
The History of New York by Diedrich Knickerbocker.
The satire was so well contrived, the fun sounded so
earnest, that a few actually believed it to be a true history. The world laughed — but the Dutch themselves
were not pleased: they did not like jokes made on
their ancestors. Irving inserted a satisfactory apol-
ogy in the next edition. His kindliness kept him
from ever giving an intentional wound; he tickled
with the feather of playful wit, but never stabbed
with the dagger of scornful hate. His modesty made
him consider the history only a merry, passing joke,
its success not turning him to a "life by literature."
He became silent partner in his brothers' firm; tried
a little politics, going to Washington and becoming
acquainted with President Madison and his wife Dolly
Madison; and kept up a little writing for magazines,
publishing a memoir of the English poet Campbell.
He thought of being a soldier, but the War of 1812
was over before he could do any fighting.

His Visit to England. — The Irving brothers
needed some one to send to Europe to watch over
their interests, and naturally Washington was the one
to go. The great poets, Moore, Byron, Coleridge,
and others, were alive then, and Scott was entranc-
ing all readers with his Waverley Novels. Such was
the society into which Irving was received with open
arms, his charming manners winning him as much
popularity in England as at home. His mind was
so filled with the best thoughts of English literature
that every cowslip, violet, or daisy was to him a

little "document of poetry." He says: "I shall never forget the thrill of ecstasy with which I first saw the lark rise almost from beneath my feet, and wing its musical flight up into the morning sky." At such sights there came to him from all the great English poets lines teeming with associations. This cultivated, delightful gentleman had talents which needed some severe shock to shake off the dust of indolence and indifference, and the shock came. These three happy years were suddenly ended by the failure of the firm of the Irving brothers. A blessed failure it was to every American reader, for it awakened all the manhood and genius Irving possessed. Refusing government situations as well as an editorship that was offered him, he went to work, determined to support not only himself but his family, and he nobly and successfully carried out the determination.

"The Sketch-book." — The first result of his exertions was *The Sketch-book*, his best and best-known book. It came out in pamphlets in the United States, and Walter Scott persuaded his English publisher to buy it for a thousand dollars. It is well named, consisting as it does of sketches, romances, and essays; the most famous is the story of Rip Van Winkle, while others very charming are *The Legend of Sleepy Hollow* and the essays on Westminster Abbey and Stratford-on-Avon. There was no fear now for Irving's future: his writings were all salable at home and in England.

"Bracebridge Hall" and "Tales of a Traveler," the former containing sketches of English life, were the productions of the next five years, and the large sum of money paid for them made him safe from poverty; but his admirers were asking something more solid than sketches and tales. His next four books, written during a three years' stay in Spain, were of a different character, except *The Alhambra*, a group of Moorish tales of that wonderful old palace, with a most fascinating description of the Alhambra itself.[1] Some of the romantic legends were composed in the building itself, for he had a room there.

His first solid work was a *Life of Columbus*, which brought him $18,000; and he ceased to spend his strength on the short stories, though they will never fail to please. By them he has made the Hudson, the Catskills, and the Alhambra literary shrines, where his readers love to wander and think of him and the legends he has told of them, just as he used to wander to those spots he had read of in English song and story. Our government recalled him from Spain to be secretary of legation in London, and there many honors were heaped upon him. He was given the gold medal of the Royal Society of Literature and the degree of D.C.L. from Oxford University; he had applause and flattering attentions. Yet in the midst of it all he sighed for home, and giving up his appointment, he came back to New York after an absence of seventeen years. He was met with such a reception as his talent deserved; but he was not hurt by the compliments, for he was always rather embarrassed by praise, and never seemed to think he deserved so much fame.

Sunnyside. — After a trip to the West through the prairies, — he wrote two volumes describing it, — he settled down at Sunnyside, "a little old-fashioned stone mansion, all made up of gable ends, and as full of angles and corners as an old cocked hat." This was near Tarrytown on the Hudson, near where

[1] Alhambra, a palace built by the Moors when they ruled Spain; it is in ruins.

André was captured, and not far from the scenes of some of Irving's earlier sketches. A widowed sister with her two daughters lived with him, and these nieces thought him the best, sweetest, jolliest uncle in all the universe. The government again sent him to Europe—as minister to Spain this time. He was far too busy with state affairs and too much afflicted with gout to think up books, but not too busy nor suffering too much to think up letters to his young nieces. And such letters! Not a word about the gout or the heavy cares of his office, but a great deal about the little thirteen-year old queen of Spain and her younger sister; a great deal too about the ribbons, laces, jewelry; all the finery of court. He said his time was "occupied in conjuring up nothings to say to little girls"—the princesses. Some of it was occupied in conjuring up bright things to say to the little girls his nieces.

His last thirteen years were spent quietly in his own study. Rich, honored, a favorite among other literary men and at the courts of Europe, yet unspoiled, unconceited, the loving, warm-hearted brother, the devoted uncle, toiled on for the sake of those he loved. *The Life of Washington*, his longest work, and the biography of Goldsmith [1] belong to this period. Ill health made him lay down his pen, but not his cheerful spirits, for he jested quaintly even of his sleepless nights. One night as his niece was smoothing his pillow he exclaimed, "When will this end?" and was dead. This was on the 28th of November, 1859.

Be sure to read Irving, not only because he is a model of good English style, always using the right

---

[1] Oliver Goldsmith, an English poet, novelist, essayist, etc., of the eighteenth century. Wrote *The Vicar of Wakefield* and the play *She Stoops to Conquer.*

word in the right place, but because of the pleasure he will give you. In his hands the most commonplace incident becomes interesting, and he is clear and simple. If you do not know of his Rip Van Winkle, who was entrapped by the mischievous sprites of the mountains and put to sleep for twenty years, hunt up *The Sketch-book*. The tale has been dramatized and acted by our finest actors. Another story that will interest you is that of Ichabod Crane, who was so frightened by the headless horseman. And *The Alhambra*, with its talking doves, its exciting adventures, is more charming than the *Arabian Nights*.

Summary. — WASHINGTON IRVING (1783–1859), first world-read American author. Born in New York; home in old age, Sunnyside. Early idle life, trips to Europe and seventeen years abroad, secretary of legation to England, minister to Spain. Chief books: *Knickerbocker's History of New York*, a burlesque; *Sketch-book ; Bracebridge Hall ; Tales of a Traveler ; The Alhambra ;* sketches, essays, and tales; *Life of Columbus ; Life of Washington ; Mahomet and his Successors ;* and *Oliver Goldsmith.*

CHAPTER VII

AMERICA'S FIRST GREAT POET — WILLIAM CULLEN BRYANT.

"**Thanatopsis.**" — In 1817 there appeared in the *North American Review* (a newly established magazine) a poem which marks the beginning of America's true poetry. This was *Thanatopsis*, and came from the brain of a young man, William Cullen Bryant, a man whose life covers three quarters of our century, but whose poetical career belongs especially to the early part.

He was born Nov. 3, 1794, at Cummington, Massachusetts, the second of seven boys and girls. His ancestors on both sides were descended from the "Mayflower" Pilgrims, and in his home the Puritan virtues of truth, fear of God, reverence, quietness, and industry were taught. From such homes many of our first great, good men inherited and acquired their greatness and goodness, though they may have missed the brightness and tenderness where there was so much stern, quiet repression. There was not an abundance of money in the Bryant household; we know that the mother did all the work, which meant spinning and weaving, as well as cooking, washing and ironing, and sewing, besides the care of her seven children. Little sentences from her diary show that she had untiring energy, and William was like her. In spite of poverty, there were books in the family and bookish tastes. Dr. Bryant, the

father, was both educated and cultivated; he taught
his son to write correct English, and to omit unnecessary words in his poems and compositions.

A Precocious Child. — William Cullen learned
wonderfully fast, and was a precocious child from
the cradle.   Before his second birthday he knew his
letters, and at four years old he was at school, fast
becoming a good reader and speller.   We wonder if
he ever made mud pies or rode stickhorses.   And
he modestly says that his brother was much brighter
than himself — a remarkable set of children!   His
gift for poetry made itself known at an early date.
In his twelfth year he composed some verses to be
recited at school — his first publication.   Even before
this I think he received his first literary earnings, a
" ninepenny piece," for having turned a chapter of
Job into verse.   At thirteen a longer poem, *The
Embargo*, a political satire, appeared in print.   Yet
these early pieces were not at all in Bryant's natural
style, for they were like the poems he had read, and
these were what is called "artificial" in style, no
Nature being in them.   And Bryant, though so unex-
citable, so cool, had one passion, and that was love
for Nature — for the mountains, the valleys, the trees,
and the flowers.   While other boys were forming ardent
friendships or having young love affairs, he was pouring out his soul in love for Nature herself.   Near his
home were grand old woods, and when he had helped
with the daily work he would wander into these forests
to hold communion with Nature and hear her speak
her various voices.   Especially did he love the grand
oak trees, and ever through his poetry do we hear
the whisper of their leaves; we hear, too, the roar of
the ocean, and all the voices of outdoor life.   His
youthful soul puzzled over the mysteries of this life,
over the never-ceasing return of fading flowers, over

the constant changes, just as many other poets had puzzled; but he had never seen the messages from these other poets. Living in England there was one poet with this same passionate devotion to Nature— William Wordsworth. Though now considered a rare genius, nearly all England ridiculed his first published works. The boy Bryant came across a volume of Wordsworth's poems, and immediately knew he had found a spirit like his own. "A thousand springs," he said, "seemed to gush up in my heart, and the face of Nature of a sudden changed into a strange freshness."

The Poet of Nature. — One of Bryant's titles is "the American Wordsworth." There is, however, a wide difference between him and Wordsworth, and Bryant is intensely American. Nearly every poem has some bit of scenery, and it is always a bit of American scenery. Of his one hundred and seventy-one poems more than half are of Nature in some of her forms; for he writes few poems of people, and does not tell us stories. This is the reason they are what children would call "solemn;" yet even one of the most solemn, *Thanatopsis*, you will enjoy if you put yourself into its spirit. It is his thoughts and wonderings put into words, especially his thoughts on life and death, for they, too, are favorite subjects with him. It means "a vision of death." He was only seventeen or eighteen when he wrote it, as he sat under a great oak, and carelessly he stuck it in a pigeonhole of his father's desk. A few years afterwards it was sent to the *North American Review*, whether by himself or his father we do not know: immediately the world recognized that another poet had been born. If Bryant had written only this, it would have stamped him as a genius. He never surpassed, or even equaled, this masterpiece.

Education. — While *Thanatopsis* was lying in his father's desk its composer was seeking to educate himself. Owing to lack of money his stay at college — Williams College — was less than a year, though a degree was conferred on him in 1819. He deserved it more than many a full graduate, so diligently had he read and studied, having taught himself several languages so thoroughly that translations from them are among his poems. At thirteen he had translated Latin verses; when seventy he gave to us a translation of Homer, the Greek bard, a fine translation too.

Being too poor to trust to the support of literary work, not yet thought of as a profession, he, like so many of our early authors, tried law. In his *Green River* he speaks of hating

"To toil for the dregs of men
And scrawl strange words with a barbarous pen."

Of course, with his heart not in it, the toil was not very successful, though he kept at it nine or ten years, publishing only one small volume during the period.

First Volume. — This volume contained his longest single poem, one delivered before the Phi Beta Kappa Society at Harvard, *The Ages*, or a vision of history; for, except his translation of Homer, Bryant undertook no long poetical work. He moved to New York in 1825, and soon became one of the editors of the New York *Evening Post*, a position which he retained for fifty years. During that long period he was a prominent figure in politics as well as in society and literature. His heavy duties left him no free hours for verse-making; only an occasional piece, therefore, appeared. Irving and all the first group of writers were his friends, as were our later groups.

Traveler and Orator. — He was an extensive traveler, visiting Europe six times and making tours over his own country. The prose volume, *Letters of a Traveler*, describes these journeyings. Often he was called upon for addresses or orations. He delivered an oration May 29, 1878, at the unveiling of a statue in Central Park, standing, as he spoke, with bared head. Overcome with the heat, he fell as he was entering a friend's house, struck the marble step, and received a blow from the effects of which he died a fortnight later. Hardly any man had been crowned with more honors or surrounded by more admiring friends. His seventieth and eightieth birthdays were made ovations by his friends.

What to Read. — *The Death of the Flowers* is beautiful; read it in November, when the dry leaves lie in heaps and the flowers are all gone. *The Forest Hymn* and *Autumn Woods* are grand; *To the Fringed Gentian* and *To a Waterfowl* are popular; *The Flood of Years* and *The Land of Dreams* are pure and dignified, as are all his poems; *Seventy-six* and *The Antiquity of Freedom* are patriotic. Especially simple and homelike is *The Planting of the Apple-tree.* His religious pieces are sweet and comforting.

Summary. — WILLIAM CULLEN BRYANT (1794–1878). Born in Massachusetts; lived near New York City; for fifty years editor of *Evening Post*. America's first great poet, a poet of Nature.

Poems: *Thanatopsis*, best; *The Ages, Death of the Flowers, The Flood of Years, To a Waterfowl, The Forest Hymn, Autumn Woods,* etc.

Translations: Homer's *Iliad* and *Odyssey.*

Prose: Letters of a Traveler. Orations, editorials.

Some Oft-quoted Lines from Bryant.

Yet not to thine eternal resting-place
Shalt thou retire alone — nor couldst thou wish

Couch more magnificent.   Thou shalt lie down
With patriarchs of the infant world — with kings,
The powerful of the earth, the wise, the good,
Fair forms, and hoary seers of ages past,
All in one mighty sepulcher. . . .
. . . And what if thou withdraw
Unheeded by the living, and no friend
Take note of thy departure?   All that breathe
Will share thy destiny.   The gay will laugh
When thou art gone, the solemn brood of care
Plod on, and each one as before will chase
His favorite phantom. . . .
So live that when thy summons comes to join
The innumerable caravan, that moves
To that mysterious realm, where each shall take
His chamber in the silent halls of death,
Thou go not like the quarry slave at night,
Scourged to his dungeon, but, sustained and soothed
By an unfaltering trust, approach thy grave
Like one who wraps the drapery of his couch
About him, and lies down to pleasant dreams.

THANATOPSIS.

Truth crushed to earth shall rise again —
    The eternal years of God are hers;
But Error, wounded, writhes in pain,
    And dies amid his worshipers.

THE BATTLE FIELD.

The melancholy days are come, the saddest of the year,
Of wailing winds, and naked woods, and meadows brown
    and sear.
Heaped in the hollows of the grove, the autumn leaves
    lie dead;
They rustle to the eddying gust, and to the rabbit's tread.

THE DEATH OF THE FLOWERS.

The groves were God's first temples.   Ere man learned
To hew the shaft, and lay the architrave,
And spread the roof above them.

A FOREST HYMN.

CHAPTER VIII.

OUR FIRST FAMOUS NOVELIST — JAMES FENIMORE
COOPER.

Stories of Adventure. — Our American ancestors had so much real fighting to do, knew so many real adventures to recount, that they felt no need of making up stories about imaginary adventures, neither did they love the real Indian enough to make any imaginary hero of him. But as life became more quiet and uneventful, readers craved stories of something more exciting than their ordinary existence. No stories were at hand except those imported from England; for only a few people could enjoy Brown's horribly ghastly tales, and he had died in 1810. But in 1820, the very year in which Sir Walter Scott finished his *Ivanhoe* and the English were praising *The Sketch-book*, Cooper, " the second writer who was to show to the world that we were to have a literature of our own," published his first novel, having been led to the attempt by a curious incident. He had never had any decided literary tastes, but had led for several years a seafaring life, and had settled down as a gentleman farmer, when he came across a certain English novel, which he considered so poor that he threw it down with the exclamation, " I could write as good a story myself." His wife may have argued the point, or may have smiled disbelievingly — he went to work and wrote one.

"The Spy." — He made the mistake of trying to

43

describe English life, of which he knew nothing, and produced a very stupid novel, of which he was heartily ashamed ; but instead of being discouraged he tried again, and in another year *The Spy*, a story of the Revolution, was ready for publication. The "spy," or hero, is Harvey Birch, a very shrewd spy and brave soldier, the story of whose adventures delighted not only America and England, but all Europe. The book was even translated into the Persian and Arabic languages. The French were particularly charmed with these new wild scenes and characters.

Pioneer Life.—Cooper knew about pioneer life, and about life among the hunters and trappers, for when he was a mere baby his father had moved from Burlington, New Jersey, to a real wilderness near Otsego Lake, New York. Here he built a large house and laid out the streets of a town, naming it Cooperstown. He had been a prominent man, both a judge and a Congressman. Few settlers came to the newly laid out town, the fields and forests still remained uncultivated, and over these James Fenimore roamed, learning the ways of Indians and fur traders, the habits of wild animals, and the secrets of wild Nature ; for he knew how to use his eyes.

At College and at Sea.—The free days in the free forest made the restraints of Yale College, whither he was sent at fourteen, unbearable. He was such an indifferent student that he could not finish the course. Lack of study shows in his books in many careless sentences and constructions. When sixteen, being dismissed from college, he shipped as a sailor. Afterwards joining the navy, he continued life on a ship six years. He married, and, either because his young wife disliked the ocean or because he had tired of it, he resigned his commission and settled first in Westchester County and afterwards in New York City.

Indian Tales.—After the success of *The Spy* his boyhood memories came to him, and he determined to write stories of the far-off days when the white man dared penetrate hardly beyond the roar of the Atlantic. He could recall the backwoods life clearly; his imagination easily filled in the true background with incident after incident. He drew well and accurately the Indian wigwam, the war council, the trail, the attack. We think of the Indian as brave, loyal, shrewd, enduring, never forgetting either a kindness or an injury, just because Cooper so shows him to us. Some people laugh and say, " Cooper's Indians and dead Indians are the only good Indians; " but he paints both good and bad red men. All Europe clings to Cooper's ideal Indian; and it was because his books were considered historical that they were so immensely popular. More real and more attractive than the Indian is Natty Bumppo, the pioneer or backwoodsman, who appears in five of his stories. These stories are called the *Leather-stocking* series, because Natty Bumppo was dubbed *Leatherstocking* by the Indians. They are *The Deer-slayer*, *The Last of the Mohicans*, *The Pathfinder*, *The Pioneers*, *The Prairie*. I never saw a boy that did not like tales of wild life, of shooting wild beasts and following trails. Natty Bumppo was so good a marksman that when he pointed his gun at an Indian or a panther it was a dead Indian or a dead panther. Yet he was a gentleman at heart, noble, true, kind hearted, and tender. Adventure is plentiful in these stories, with nothing that will hurt your heart or soul.

Sea Stories.—Just as stirring as the *Leatherstock-ing Tales* are his sea stories, for here, too, Cooper knew what he was describing. A dispute led to the writing of these: having contended that Scott's *Pirate*

was not so good as it would have been if Scott had
been a sailor, he wrote, to prove his point, a sea
novel, *The Pilot*.   One of the characters, Long Tom
Coffin, a veteran sailor, is as fine a specimen of rough
manhood as Natty Bumppo.   The scenes are laid
during the Revolution, and John Paul Jones, who
fought so gallantly in many a sea fight of the Revolution, is one of the characters in the story.   *The Red
Rover* is another sea novel.   Both are full of stirring
accounts of naval battles, of storms, shipwrecks, fires,
and the like.

Other Works. — These were not Cooper's only
works, for he produced more than thirty; but only
nine or ten are worthy of acquaintance.   Many of his
later works are tedious and uninteresting.   We remember them because they were written by the author of
the *Leatherstocking Tales*, and not because of any
merit of their own.   Cooper's neglect of his studies at
school and his rapid, careless work injured his style.
Unlike Irving, he often gets "the wrong word in the
wrong place;" but he is fresh and lively, picturing what
his imagination sees, and what no other imagination
had seen, so plainly that the reader can see it too.
The title "the American Walter Scott" is deserved
by him.

Two Southern Writers. — Of course Cooper's
popularity set other people to writing on the same
class of subjects.   Two Southern novelists, William
Gilmore Simms and John Pendleton Kennedy, have
written stories of Revolutionary or Colonial times.
Kennedy's three novels, *Swallow Barn*, *Horseshoe
Robinson*, and *Rob of the Bowl*, describe country life
in Virginia and South Carolina in the Revolution, and
in Maryland during Colonial days.   All are found
only in old libraries, tucked away probably behind
more recent books.   Kennedy's career in politics —

for he held different offices—soon put the writing of novels out of his thoughts.   William Gilmore Simms struggled to found a Southern literature, but the small number of inhabitants scattered over a large territory furnished not enough readers.   Before the war immense plantations and households of numerous slaves engrossed the attention of the wealthy country gentlemen.   Genius and talents were given to oratory, politics, statesmanship, but it was hardly considered an honorable employment to write for money.   Therefore Simms undertook a hopeless task, and he wrote too much to perfect his work, and tried too hard to invent extraordinary or exciting incidents to take a very high rank.   *The Scout, The Wigwam and the Cabin*, and *The Maroon* tell by their names the character of his narratives.   *Yemassee* is his best story. Poems and histories also came from his pen.

Herman Melville. — Four wildly exciting tales of adventure might be named here; they are of just the kind to please the boys.   They are *Typee, Omoo, White Jacket*, and *Moby Dick, or the White Whale*, all by Herman Melville.   Melville having deserted from a whaling ship was kept for months by cannibals on the Marquesas Islands.   The first two volumes tell of life among the cannibals; the third, of life on a man-of-war; the fourth describes the chase of a huge white whale called Moby Dick—it had maimed a whaling captain, who had sworn to revenge himself on the animal.

A True Story of Adventure. —Though hardly belonging here,—for it is not fiction but truth,— *Two Years before the Mast* may be included in this chapter.   It is by Richard Henry Dana, Jr., and gives an account of a voyage to California by way of Cape Horn, the writer having gone out as a sailor in quest of better health.   The trip was made in the year 1833 or about that time, and is as interesting to-day as it was then.

Summary.—JAMES FENIMORE COOPER (1789–1851), from New York, first well-known novelist. Wrote more than thirty volumes : *Leatherstocking Tales,* five novels of pioneer and Indian life; *The Pilot* and *Red Rover,* sea stories; *The Spy,* Revolutionary story.

Two Southern Novelists: John Pendleton Kennedy (1795–1870), *Swallow Barn, Horseshoe Robinson,* and *Rob of the Bowl;* William Gilmore Simms (1806–70), South Carolina, poet, novelist, and miscellaneous writer; *Yemassee,* best work.

Herman Melville (1819–92), *Typee, Omoo, White Jacket,* and *Moby Dick, or the White Whale,* stories of adventure.

Richard Henry Dana, Jr. (1815–82), *Two Years before the Mast,* a true account of a voyage to California by way of Cape Horn.

CHAPTER IX.

Half-forgotten Authors. — As soon as one great author arises minor authors appear, and they naturally drift to the same literary center. During Colonial times Boston was the center, during Revolutionary times Hartford, Connecticut, and the first thirty years of this century New York was the home of literary men and literary periodicals. Of the New York group only three are really famous — Irving, Cooper, and Bryant; but thanks are due to the less conspicuous writers too, for they tried to create an American literature, and by their own efforts, and the efforts they aroused in others, they did give an impulse to our native literature. In their own day they were extensively read and extravagantly praised; in our day one or two poems from them or about them are all that recall them. We forget our debt to them.

There is one common feature several writers of this period possessed: they did not fulfill the brilliant promise they seemed to give. There are several possible reasons for this disappointment: they may have been overrated by friends; they turned their attention to other things, as to business, and business and poetry are not congenial — the Muse of poetry soon fled from the clink of dollars in New York to more quiet shades; but the chief reason is that we demand more to-day from writers than was demanded of them then — people were not critical, and were pleased with poems which we now consider common-place or shallow, though they did far excel those of the two other periods studied.

Paulding, Drake, and Halleck.—Irving's friend, James K. Paulding, amused his readers by his *Diverting History of John Bull and Brother Jonathan* and his *Dutchman's Fireside;* was associated, too, with one or two periodicals, and was prominent politically.

Joseph Rodman Drake and Fitz-Greene Halleck are always mentioned together, for their friendship was like that of David and Jonathan. Together they wrote bright society squibs called the *Croaker Papers*, and Drake wrote the well known poem entitled *The American Flag*, beginning :

> " When Freedom from her mountain height
>   Unfurled her standard to the air,
>   She tore the azure robes of night,
>   And set the stars of glory there."

How the boys used to recite that, using their most triumphant gestures in the lines :

> " Flag of the brave ! *thy* folds shall fly, . . .
>   Flag of the seas ! on ocean wave," etc.

One of Drake's longer poems, *The Culprit Fay*, is a dainty little fancy. He had asserted that the rivers and mountains of America would afford just the scenes to put in poetry or stories. To prove it he describes in this piece fairyland, placing it on the Hudson ; for any one can recognize from his description the neighborhood. The fay has committed the crime of falling in love with a mortal maiden. Being tried by the other fairies he is punished, and part of the sentence is that he must light his lamp from the last faint spark of a shooting star. The whole adventure is vividly told. At the early age of twenty-five

Drake died of consumption. His memory was embalmed by Halleck in verses that keep both men unforgotten. The two lines —

> " None knew thee but to love thee,
> None named thee but to praise,"

are as often repeated as any two lines in our language. Besides this memorial poem Halleck has given us other oft-quoted stanzas. Many children have been drilled on his *Marco Bozzaris*, especially on the hero's cheer to his band :

> " Strike ! till the last armed foe expires;
> Strike ! for your altars and your fires;
> Strike ! for the green graves of your sires,
> God, and your native land ! "

There are a few other pieces by Halleck — one on Red-Jacket, an Indian chief, and one on Burns, the Scottish poet — that are still popular. His statue stands in Central Park, New York, and at its unveiling Whittier recited a poem that tells how —

> " In common ways, with common men,
> He served his race and time
> As well as if his clerkly pen
> Had never danced to rhyme."

He was a clerk in Astor's office, and had no care for poetic fame.

Another pair of friends were Samuel Woodworth and George P. Morris, each known now by one song, *The Old Oaken Bucket* and *Woodman, Spare that Tree*. They founded a literary paper, the New York *Mirror*, which did good in bringing out new writers and encouraging a love of reading.

Nathaniel P. Willis. — Among those who wrote for the *Mirror* was a young man who about 1830 was considered one of the shining lights of literature — a writer who was written about, admired, criticised, and whose pieces were copied far and wide. This was Nathaniel P. Willis, whose works are now scarcely read at all, though old people still speak of him with respect. If a poor poet himself, he brought out and encouraged other writers, and in his anxiety for the spread of books, papers, knowledge, he helped the cause of literature in this country. He had fine opportunities for a literary life. His father founded, it is claimed, the first religious newspaper in the world, and it was in this that the son published his poems on Bible events, as *The Death of Absalom*, etc. Willis went to New York to be associate editor of the *Mirror*, and was sent to Europe to write sketches for it. These were well named *Pencilings by the Way*. He was the first special newspaper correspondent and the first interviewer, and a paper which he and George P. Morris established, *The Home Journal*, is still in existence.

" **Peter Parley**," whose histories used to be such a delight to young people, was doing his best work at this time. The name is that which was chosen by a Boston publisher, Samuel G. Goodrich. He was one of the first to remember the boys and girls, and he published for them nearly two hundred books — not all compiled by himself, however; for he employed different writers, and among them Willis. It was before children had many books written especially for them, and hence they loved " Peter Parley " almost as well as children nowadays love Santa Claus.

A New England poet, prose writer, and artist of this period, Washington Allston, did much to promote culture, and was considered a remarkable genius. He influenced more by his talk and ideas than by his pen, for he left nothing written worthy of mention.   He was our first great painter.   Allston's brother-in-law, Richard Henry Dana, Sr., was a member of the Anthology Club, a club of literary men at Cambridge, whose members founded the *North American Review* in 1815.   Dana edited it for some time.   *The Buccaneer* is his best poem.   Orestes Augustus Brownson was the founder of the *Boston Quarterly Review*, afterwards called *Brownson's*,—the first American periodical reprinted in England.

Authors of Single Poems.—An effort was made to have a drama of our own, but to this day America has to send abroad for her finest plays to be acted in theater and opera.   One playwright, John Howard Payne, composed many plays, but lives in our hearts to-day for one song, *Home, Sweet Home*, which was in one of his plays.   Other poets are remembered for just one piece: Francis Scott Key for his *Star-spangled Banner;* Richard Henry Wilde for *My Life is Like the Summer Rose;* Philip Pendleton Cooke for *Florence Vane;* and Clement C. Moore for *A Visit from St. Nicholas*, beginning

" 'Twas the night before Christmas, and all through the   house."

Summary.—*New York Group :* James K. Paulding (1779–1860), *The Diverting History of John Bull and Brother Jonathan.*   Joseph Rodman Drake (1795–1820), *Culprit Fay.*   Fitz-Greene Halleck (1790–1867), *Marco Bozzaris*, lines on Drake, on Burns.   Samuel Woodworth (1785–1842), *The Old Oaken Bucket.*   George P. Morris (1802–64), *Woodman, Spare that Tree.*   John Howard Payne (1792–1852), playwright; *Home, Sweet Home.*   Clement C. Moore (1779–1863), *A Visit from St. Nicholas.*   Nathaniel P. Willis (1806–1867), poet and prose writer.

Southern Poets: Francis Scott Key (1780–1843), *The Star-spangled Banner.* Richard Henry Wilde (1789–1847), *My Life is Like the Summer Rose.* Philip Pendleton Cooke (1816–1850), *Florence Vane;* wrote also *Froissart Ballads.*

New England Authors: Washington Allston (1779–1843), poet, painter, and prose writer; *The Sylphs of the Seasons, Lectures on Art.* Richard Henry Dana, Sr. (1787–1879), poet and prose writer, editor of *North American Review;* best poem, *The Buccaneer.* Samuel G. Goodrich ("Peter Parley") (1793–1860) published books for children. Orestes Augustus Brownson (1803–1876), founder of *Boston Quarterly Review.*

Some Stanzas from Drake's "Culprit Fay."

'Tis the hour of fairy ban and spell:
The wood-tick has kept the minutes well;
He has counted them all with click and stroke
Deep in the heart of the mountain-oak,
And he has awakened the sentry elve
   Who sleeps with him in the haunted tree,
To bid him ring the hour of twelve,
    And call the fays to their revelry;
Twelve small strokes on his tinkling bell
('Twas made of the white snail's pearly shell):
Midnight comes and all is well!
Hither, hither wing your way!
'Tis the dawn of the fairy-day.

   .   .   .   .   .   .

They come from beds of lichen green,
They creep from the mullein's velvet screen;
Some on the backs of beetles fly
   From the silver tops of moon-touched trees,
Where they swung in their cobweb hammocks high,
    And rocked about in the evening breeze; . . .
  .   .   . In the tricksy pomp of fairy pride.

   .   .   .   .

He puts his acorn helmet on ;
It was plumed of the silk of the thistle-down ;
The corselet plate that guarded his breast
Was once the wild bee's golden vest ;
His cloak, of a thousand mingled dyes,
Was formed of the wings of butterflies ;
His shield was the shell of a lady-bug queen,
Studs of gold on a ground of green ;
And the quivering lance which he brandished bright
Was the sting of a wasp he had slain in fight.
Swift he bestrode his fire-fly steed ;
   He bared his blade of the bent glass blue ;
He drove his spurs of the cockle seed,
   And away like a glance of thought he flew
To skim the heavens and follow far
The fiery trail of the rocket star.

Oft-heard Lines from Halleck.

For thou art freedom's now, and fame's, —
One of the few immortal names
   That were not born to die.
MARCO BOZZARIS.

Praise to the bard ! his words are driven,
   Like flower seeds by the far winds sown,
Where'er beneath the sky of heaven
   The birds of fame have flown.

Praise to the man ! the nation stood
   Beside his coffin with wet eyes, —
Her brave, her beautiful, her good, —
   As when a loved one dies.

Such graves as his are pilgrim shrines,
   Shrines to no code or creed confined, —
The Delphian vales, the Palestines,
   The Meccas of the mind.
ON BURNS.

CHAPTER X.

Born in Boston, adopted in Virginia, educated partly in England, connected with Southern and Northern magazines, a writer of weird tales, yet always thought of as a poet, Edgar Allan Poe belongs to no group ; he is emphatically "one to himself." The date even of his birth is a disputed point, but Jan. 19, 1809, is generally accepted. Both his parents were actors, who died in Richmond within a few days of each other, leaving this boy of two or three years of age. His godparents, kind, wealthy people of Richmond, named Allan, adopted him, and, as they were childless, they treated him as their own son, giving him every advantage.

School Life.— He was sent to an English school the first five years of school life, another five years he attended a private academy in Richmond, then went to the University of Virginia. There he gambled and made bad debts until he was finally taken away by his foster-father, who placed him in his own counting room. A quarrel with Mr. Allan made him start out as his own master. It was the year 1827, when Greece was struggling against Turkey. Lord Byron, the English poet, had offered himself to Greece, and had died on her shores. Poe professed a wish to imitate him, but instead of going to Greece he enlisted as a private in the U. S. Army under the name of Edgar A. Perry.

First Volume.—The next year he returned to Richmond, published his first volume of poems, made friends with Mr. Allan, secured an appointment at West Point, and studied so well for a few months that he seemed to have turned a new leaf; but he again drifted into idleness and drinking habits, and, in 1831, was expelled. A love affair led to a final quarrel with his adopted father; he had to rely at last on his own resources.

Literary Successes.—Going to Baltimore, he chose literature as a profession, and began the career by winning a hundred-dollar prize for a short tale, *A Manuscript found in a Bottle*. He was given the editorship of the *Southern Literary Messenger*, and a salary of $520 a year. His strange tales and unusual critical notices began to make him famous; he married his beautiful cousin, Virginia Clemm—she is the "Annabel Lee" of the poem; and there was promise of both success and happiness for his future life. But his fickleness, quarrelsomeness, and drinking habits made both impossible. He was first engaged with one magazine, then another; first at one place, then another. Even when he had increased the circulation of a periodical he would suddenly leave it to drift to some other, generally quarreling with the publishers before he left. A magazine of his own which he undertook failed completely. At about the same time his wife, a consumptive invalid, died—a sorrow from which he never recovered. His lectures and criticisms on other poets were so unkind that they made for him many enemies. Yet he had the power to win success. London was talking about him. A story of Paris, *The Murders in the Rue Morgue*, was so warmly received in France that the French people have since liked him better than any other American author. The explanation of both his unpopularity as a man and of his popularity as a writer is perhaps to be found in the fact that his imagination was out of proportion to all his other faculties. It is the kindest reason we can give for his fickleness, his ugly humor, and his untruths. He imagined that a change would be an improvement; he imagined that he had been badly treated; he imagined that what he said was true. Not all his sixty tales are good. He failed in his attempts to be funny or anything out of the gloomy, fantastic line. Twenty of his stories are especially liked, and can be read and re-read. *The Gold Bug, The Black Cat, Hans Pfaal, A Tale of the Ragged Mountains, Ligeia,* and *The Purloined Letter* are a few. The last is a detective story, Poe being the first to write detective stories. There is no moral, no lesson in anything he gave us — his own sad story is a moral lesson.

"The Raven." — Ever since Jan. 29, 1845, Poe has been to the world a poet, not a prose writer, for that day there was published in the *Evening Mirror*, the poem entitled *The Raven*. Europeans sometimes speak as if this were our only poem: there has never been another just like it. Whatever else *The Raven* may mean — for many attempts have been made to explain it — it is a "poem of despair." The poet pondering at midnight, seeking from books "surcease of sorrow — sorrow for the lost Lenore," is startled by a tapping at his chamber door. "When he open flung the shutter" "in there stepped a stately raven," and this "ghastly, grim, and ancient raven" perched itself on a bust above his door. Smiling, the poet asked the bird its name.

"Quoth the Raven, 'Nevermore!'"

Again and again, as if in answer to his wild **won-**

derings and his questionings if there was any balm
in Gilead to comfort him for his lost Lenore—

> "Quoth the Raven, 'Nevermore!'"

until the man shrieked:

> "'Take thy beak from out my heart, and take thy form
>   from off my door!'
>   Quoth the Raven, 'Nevermore!'
> And the Raven, never flitting, still is sitting, still is sit-
>   ting
> On the pallid bust of Pallas, just above my chamber
>   door;
> And his eyes have all the seeming of a demon that is
>   dreaming,
> And the lamplight o'er him streaming throws his shadow
>   on the floor;
> And my soul from out that shadow that lies floating on
>   the floor
>   Shall be lifted—*nevermore!*"

Poe had the rare gift of fitting words and meaning together musically. This might be expected from
his theory of poetry: "Music is the perfection of the
soul or idea of poetry; the vagueness of exaltation
is precisely what we should aim at in poetry." He
strictly followed this rule: a vague exaltation most
pleasing to the ear is in all his poetry. *The Bells*
illustrates his power over the sound of words: in his
description of

> "The sledges with the bells, —
>   Silver bells,"

we can hear

> "The tintinnabulation that so musically wells,"

28

> "They tinkle, tinkle, tinkle
>   In the icy air of night."

Just as plainly do we distinguish

> " The mellow wedding bells, —
>   Golden bells ! "

for

> " From the molten-golden notes
>   What a liquid ditty floats !
> What a gush of euphony voluminously wells ! "

And " the ear distinctly tells," " by the twanging and the clanging," " in the jangling and the wrangling," " in the clamor and the clangor,"

> " The loud alarum bells, —
>   Brazen bells ! "

There is a " melancholy menace " in the tolling of the bells, —

> " Iron bells ! "

for he has made us hear the " muffled monotone " of " their moaning and their groaning."

Of his forty poems five are the property of all, are familiar to all ; ten or a dozen, all short, are worth knowing. *Israfel, Ulalume, Dreamland, The Haunted Palace,* and *To Helen* are among these. He might have done far more, but death came. Some say he was on his way to be married to a Virginia poetess ; some say she had rejected him : we know he was taken with delirium tremens and died at a hospital at Baltimore in October, 1849. Poor Poe ! sensitive, high-tempered, capricious, he never overcame his spoiled-child ways and willfulness. Pityingly we drop a tear over the grave of one who, whether slandered or overpraised, has ever had one word, " Genius," appended to his name. Critics have gone further and named him "America's greatest, only poetical genius."

Summary.— EDGAR ALLAN POE (1809–49), from
    Virginia, writer of weird tales and a poet.

*Tales: The Gold Bug, The Black Cat, Hans Pfaal,
    The Purloined Letter.*   Detective and ghost
    stories.

Poems: The Raven, Annabel Lee, The Bells, Israfel,
    and *To Helen.*   Wrote criticisms.   Most orig-
    inal of all our writers; of wonderful imagi-
    nation; has a strange charm not easy to explain.
    A sad, bad life, ending in a hospital, where he
    died of delirium tremens.

From Annabel Lee.

It was many and many a year ago,
    In a kingdom by the sea,
That a maiden lived whom you may know
    By the name of Annabel Lee;
And this maiden she lived with no other thought
    Than to love and be loved by me.

I was a child and she was a child,
    In this kingdom by the sea;
But we loved with a love that was more than love,
    I and my Annabel Lee, —
With a love that the winged seraphs of heaven
    Coveted her and me.

And this was the reason that long ago,
    In this kingdom by the sea,
A wind blew out of a cloud, chilling
    My beautiful Annabel Lee;
So that her high-born kinsman came,
    And bore her away from me,
To shut her up in a sepulcher,
    In his kingdom by the sea.

CHAPTER XI.

OUR GREATEST NOVELIST—NATHANIEL HAWTHORNE.

Hawthorne's Genius.—"Some critics have affirmed that the glorious title 'Genius' belongs to only two of America's sons; none have questioned that it belongs to Hawthorne before all others." This was written of Nathaniel Hawthorne, whose tales have a mysteriousness as original as any of Poe's, but of a different character entirely. Cooper takes us into a new world among the Indians and trappers; Hawthorne takes us into the marvelous world of the human heart. He is the creator of a new style of story, one which he calls a "romance"—but it is not the romance of other authors.

Childhood.—He was born on the 4th of July, 1804, in Salem, Massachusetts, where the witches had been tortured, hanged, and burned a century before. His ancestors, very stern and gloomy Puritans, had probably helped in persecuting Quakers and ferreting out witches. Those old deeds took deep possession of Hawthorne's thoughts, as can be plainly seen in his novels. His father, a retired sea-captain,—for there had been wild seafaring men in the family,—was a very quiet, melancholy man, who died when his little boy was only four. His mother, a beautiful, dignified woman, shut herself up after her husband's death, and would have nothing to do with the outside world. Nathaniel, a handsome, healthy, mischievous lad, went to school to a private tutor, reading more than he

62

studied, especially allegories, *Pilgrim's Progress* being his particular favorite. On his reaching the age of twelve they moved to his uncle's place near Lake Sebago, Maine, as lonely a spot as can be imagined. The boy was absolutely without any companions. His amusements were hunting, walking, and skating. Sometimes he would skate by himself until midnight. His thoughts and a few books were his only company ; to amuse himself he edited a little paper of his own.

College Life. — This manner of living did not prepare him to make quick or intimate friendships when he went to Bowdoin College, Maine. Longfellow was a classmate, but Franklin Pierce, of another class, and Horatio Bridge were the students nearest to him. Bridge was the one friend to whom he opened his heart somewhat. In their after letters to each other we catch glimpses of their schooldays : of Hawthorne walking in the pines near the college, talking of what his future should be, and of Bridge encouraging him with prophecies of his coming fame. It was long years before the prophecies seemed near fulfillment. At college, though liking Greek and Latin, he had no ambition to take high rank, and on leaving Bowdoin he went back to his home in Salem and shut himself up with his mother and two sisters in utter seclusion.

From the age of twenty-one to thirty-three he was almost a hermit. All day he stayed in his room, reading, thinking, writing, not walking out until night. In the summer he sometimes made an excursion to the woods of New Hampshire ; once or twice he visited his friend Bridge ; but, with these exceptions, the twelve years appear to be one blank of solitude. He himself was afraid of the effect, but it was in this loneliness that he was shaping his style, so unique

in its character.   Though he wrote much, only forty-
five stories remain to us of that long period.   His
first novel, published at his own expense, was a failure, and was withdrawn; but it was his preparation
time in which he gathered materials for the after
period.   Americans rarely give a genius the chance
to let the products of his brain ripen: Hawthorne
had ample time, and the fruit has no touch of green
crudeness.

Some of his tales came out in periodicals; but
nobody noticed them, read them, or criticised them,
until a lady living near guessed Hawthorne to be the
author of a sketch, *The Gentle Boy.*   A few years
afterwards he married·this lady's sister, Miss Sophia
Peabody; for he began to come out of his seclusion.
The marriage was an unusually happy one, the husband and wife being entirely sufficient to each other.

Brook Farm and Some of his Earlier Works.
—Before he married, Hawthorne resided for a while
at Brook Farm, a community of literary people who
made an experiment of living together, of which you
will hear in another chapter.   He was disgusted
with his experience, but out of it his imagination
made one of his great novels, *The Blithedale Romance.*   After his marriage he moved to a building
in Concord, the " old manse " of which he writes so
delightfully in his *Mosses from an Old Manse,* a
collection of sketches.   Another volume of his short
sketches, *Twice-told Tales,* was praised by Longfellow, and was slowly recognized by others as good.
He wrote a good many sketches for children, some
of the early ones being in *Grandfather's Chair,* true
stories of real men, and one being *The Snow Image,*
a very imaginative story of a little snow-girl which
some children had made.   She becomes alive and
plays with the children, until the father, who thinks

her only a poor, frozen-looking child, insists on her being brought to the fire : of course she melts.   Other stories are in the same volume.

Stories for Children. — He was one of the people employed by Goodrich to write histories for the little folks, and *Peter Parley's Universal History* was his production.   He took as much pains with his children's books as with those for older people.   After he was distinguished he wrote *The Wonder Book* and *Tanglewood Tales* for boys and girls.   They are simple stories of mythology, and make Grecian history more interesting and Latin reading easier to understand, for they tell the old myths believed by the Greeks and Romans, and to which you often find allusions in books and papers in our own tongue.

"The Scarlet Letter." — Not making money enough by writing to support his family, Hawthorne twice had to take a place in the Salem Custom House.   When he lost his office as surveyor of the port, he went home very much discouraged.   His wife brought forth a sum of money she had saved from her housekeeping fund.   With his anxiety relieved for the present, and with his greater leisure, he could work on a novel.   The next year one of the world's greatest romances, *The Scarlet Letter*, was published, and settled forever the question of his success and his great talents.   America has produced nothing else like it.   *The Scarlet Letter* is sometimes called a " novel ; " sometimes a " romance," Hawthorne calling his works " romances."   A novel is a story, and should " tell of ordinary and probable events."   Romances can tell of marvelous circumstances, and have " a plan airily and artfully removed " from our common, everyday life.   Hawthorne's stories (for grown people) generally have some mystery in them which he keeps on hinting at and never tells plainly ; but his great power is that he shows us right down into the human heart and conscience. There is nearly always some character suffering agonies of conscience; for he shows the dreadful consequences of sin as few others can. This makes his books sad, though there is a kind humor running through their pages.

Other Novels. — After *The Scarlet Letter* appeared and everybody was eager for more from such an author, Hawthorne reaped the reward for all those lonely, discouraging days during which he had thought, brooded upon, written, and rewritten his pieces. He quickly put his thoughts on paper now, and *The House of the Seven Gables* and *The Blithedale Romance* soon followed. He was able to purchase a little home called The Wayside at Concord. His former friend Franklin Pierce being a candidate for the Presidency, he wrote a campaign biography of him. Pierce, after his election as President, sent Hawthorne as consul to England. He was away from the United States six years, traveling in France and Italy after his office was given up. While abroad he wrote another great novel, *The Marble Faun*. The scenes are laid in Italy, and a beautiful statue in Rome gave the name. On his return to The Wayside he described some of his English experiences in *Our Old Home*, a volume of sketches, not a novel.

"The Dolliver Romance." — His mind was now brooding over a romance, over several romances in fact, for an incident connected with The Wayside had taken possession of his thoughts — a legend of an old man who had tried to prepare a mixture which might keep him from dying. But bad health and a sad heart over the war kept Hawthorne from finishing the stories, though *The Dolliver Romance* was partly written, and its publication even begun in the *Atlantic Monthly*. To benefit his health he went on a trip to the White Mountains with ex-President Pierce, and on May 19, 1864, was found dead in his bed at the hotel where they were stopping. Many of our great men were present at his funeral. In the coffin lay the unfinished manuscript of his *Dolliver Romance*. The light of a great genius had gone suddenly out. Since his death his note-books have been published, notes he jotted down in America and in England, in France and in Italy.

Peculiarities of Hawthorne's Works.—All of his stories are strange and mysterious; all have the shadow of some crime, sometimes a crime committed by ancestors, not by the characters themselves. In nearly all there is repentance—and love and repentance remove the curse. There is often a hidden but plainly seen allegory. The one point in which he excels is his style, so exquisitely perfect in form, so simple, so delicate, that sentence after sentence stays in our memory both because of the thought and because of the fitting words which frame the thought. The term "literary *artist*" belongs to him as to no other writer. He took the leisure and the infinite labor to correct, polish, and repolish. He was not like his Daffydowndilly, who ran away from Master Toil.

Summary.—NATHANIEL HAWTHORNE (1804–64), Salem, Massachusetts, America's greatest novelist.
Greatest Works: Scarlet Letter (1850), *Marble Faun, House of the Seven Gables, Blithedale Romance.*
Romances, Sketches, and Tales: Twice-told Tales, Mosses from an Old Manse, Our Old Home.
For Children: Grandfather's Chair, Snow Image and other Stories, Tanglewood Tales, The Wonder Book.

CHAPTER XII

Changes of Thought in New England. — The whirlpool of business and politics in New York soon absorbed the chief attention of men who might otherwise have been great writers, and hence we find that our next group of authors hails from New England. Wonderful changes had stirred up the hearts and minds of the people in this section, changes you will have to understand somewhat before you study the literature of the period. These changes were along three lines, — religious, literary, and political, — the three going side by side, or one right after the other, and the leaders in one being nearly always active in the other two. The political movement belongs to secular history, and will be spoken of more fully in another chapter; the religious belongs to the history of the church and of theology. The first change was in theology, and we have to go back to Puritanism to explain it.

The Unitarian Movement. — Before the Revolution a man's religious beliefs were considered so very important that it was thought to be a wicked thing not to know and believe the doctrines of the church as told and retold in sermons and books. Some of these doctrines and laws seemed too gloomy and severe to a good many of the next generation. They wanted a freer, more joyous system. A new church, the Unitarian, arose and attracted to itself hundreds and thousands. From 1815 to 1830 Unitarianism was the uppermost question in New England, and Harvard College, from being a stronghold of Puritanism, became a Unitarian stronghold. I shall not attempt to tell you what Unitarianism means, and but for its effect on literature it would not be mentioned here any more than Presbyterianism or Methodism. Some of its doctrines are that man is not totally wicked by nature; that he can find God easily, "his reason apprehending Him;" and that man's duty *to man* is of chief import, the Puritans having laid stress on man's duty *to God*. It was this last belief that induced Unitarians to begin and carry on all manner of reforms that seemed likely to benefit the world. Their preachers were often just as influential in other matters as in religion.

William Ellery Channing. — Their great leader was the Rev. William Ellery Channing, whose sermons give a history of the religious controversy. Of a bright, happy piety, he was listened to as though his voice were that of an angel. His Boston pulpit was a power, and he helped others whose books are read the world over. A lecturer, orator, poet, he wrote on topics pertaining to literature, and loved to speak on practical reforms, such as the elevation of the laboring classes, etc. His essay on Milton is his best; his lecture on *Self-Culture* is fine and helpful. His successor, the Rev. Theodore Parker, finally left the Unitarian Church to found a church of his own, threw himself into politics, especially into the question of slavery, was deeply interested in such topics as poverty and temperance, and was such an enthusiastic member of a famous literary club, the "Transcendental Club," that he may be considered, first of all, a "Transcendentalist."

Transcendentalism. — "Transcendental" is a

nickname given to a club of intellectual friends who
met to discuss such deep and lofty themes that most
people would not understand their meaning if I were
to mention them.   Indeed, that is the reason this
nickname was given.   "Transcend" means "to go
beyond," and it was said that the club thought and
talked of things far beyond the comprehension of ordinary mortals, and that the members were too lofty
for earth and earthly affairs.   They really tried to in-
duce people to think less of making money, of eating
and drinking and bodily pleasures, and to think more
of Nature, and to live more in accordance with Nature's laws and less by the rules of society.   The club
originated in Boston, which had now become a center of thought; but it met so often at the little village
of Concord that it is associated with that place, and
has often been called the "Concord Club."   It lasted
only three years, breaking up by mutual consent.
The best thoughts of the meetings the members tried
to preserve in a periodical called *The Dial*, which
lasted another three years.   Transcendentalism was
really a very important movement, for it changed the
character of our literature and philosophy not a little.
It was the second step of which Unitarianism was the
first, and it had for its object the calling of the American people from their chase after wealth and material
prosperity, and the urging of them to a more sub-
stantial progress in brains, feelings, and culture.   The
Transcendentalists wished to make the world over in
many respects.

The Brook Farm Experiment. — Dissatisfied
with the existing state of society, many plans were
made to reform it.   The most famous scheme was that
of the Brook Farm, a community which the Transcendentalists established among themselves.   Property was to be held in common, and each individual.

was to share in the work, the time being divided between leisure, labor, and literature. Seventy men and women bought a place and named it "Brook Farm Institute of Agriculture and Education." The members farmed, did the chores, taught Latin and Greek, prepared literary essays, and edited a paper among themselves; but most of all they talked and talked and talked, discussing high topics of society, religion, education, and philosophy. A fire which destroyed some of the buildings broke up the community at the end of five years. Some of its members, like Hawthorne, were disappointed from the first, and had already withdrawn. It could not have lasted many more years, and yet it had an influence far more lasting than itself.

There were many other communities and joint affairs, and hundreds of pet schemes for making the earth a Garden of Eden. There was much restlessness in Europe, and its influence had crossed over to us. One new religious belief led to other new religious beliefs until there were isms innumerable. Mormonism arose, the Shakers came into prominence, and spiritualism flourished. Frightened schoolgirls were watching tables walk, and were trying to find out, through mysterious rappings and writings, what kind of men their future husbands would be. Men were going about telling the exact date of the judgment day, and wildly exciting their disciples. Everything went to prove that

"When men get loose in their theology,
The screws get started up in everything."

The whole period has well been named "the Newness." A favorite text was: "Old things are passed away; all things are become new." It seemed for

a while as if all old things — old ideas, old beliefs, old
ways — were really passing away forever.   In the
practice of medicine a new method arose; phre-
nology was all the rage as a new science; mesmerism
attracted great attention.   Some reformers went so
far as to insist that it was a sin to eat animal food;
others argued that only linen clothes should be worn;
and still others declared that no laws ought to be
obeyed.   Every manner of absurdity was taught,
and plenty of fanatics were found to believe in every
new folly that was advocated.

Results of "the Newness."— Yet out of this
ferment there resulted a quickening of thought, which
led to more reading and studying.   Much of the literature of the time, like the wild schemes, sank out
of memory; but there went out from Brook Farm
men and women who scattered the thoughts gathered
from the meeting together of the gifted people who
had made up that remarkable community.   Seven of
these people are well known for their writings: Hawthorne, Emerson, and Thoreau, who lived at Concord, and Channing, Parker, Alcott, and Margaret
Fuller.   Emerson was the master mind of the Transcendentalists.   Of Hawthorne you have already
learned, and though he is counted among this group
he does not belong to it in sympathy.   He alone
did not join in the next movement, abolitionism, or
in the struggle against slavery.   All other ideas were
soon thrown aside to fight for this cause.   This was
the political movement.

Amos Bronson Alcott was a queer, kindly visionary who had strange notions about many things, as
education, discipline, etc.   Never able to support
himself and family, his friends helped him by estab-
lishing for him " conversations," at which he talked
on high topics; and then he used to make rustic

fences and arbors for amusement and profit. Emerson was his friend, and in his *Concord Days* and *Tablets* Alcott gives an interesting account of Emerson. It was Alcott who named *The Dial*, and he was one of the contributors. Young people will be interested in the fact that he was the father of Louisa M. Alcott, who gave them *Little Women* and so many other charming books. She has given a very funny account of one of her father's experiments at Fruitlands, which was a small Brook Farm over again. "Slump Apple Farm " she said would be a more appropriate name, so complete was its failure.

Henry David Thoreau was just as eccentric as Alcott. Taking a dislike to society, he went out to Walden Pond and built with his own hands a hut ten by fifteen feet, where he lived two years. He was very poor, eking out his support by making pencils; but he needed little, for his two years at Walden Pond cost him only $68.76. Professing to despise civilized ways, he would sometimes go off with the Indians into the Maine woods for weeks together. His passion was a love for Nature. Birds, beasts, and flowers seemed to know this love, and would give up their secrets to him. The squirrels would play on his shoulders, the partridges would peep into his hut; even the fish in the pond appeared to be tame. He learned from every stone, weed, and blossom, and teaches us in his writings the lessons he has thus learned, making us see nature better and understand her more fully. The spirit of human independence breathes through every word. *Walden* is his best known work. His few scattered poems have some warm admirers. Five of his works were not published until after his death. He, Hawthorne, and Emerson sleep in the same cemetery. A pile of stones marks the site of his hut, every visitor adding a stone.

Margaret Fuller.—The most remarkable thing about Margaret Fuller, afterwards Margaret Fuller Ossoli, was that she, being a woman, should take such an active part in the new movement. For women at that time had not the opportunities for education which they have now. They were home-keepers. Margaret Fuller from early childhood had a taste for books. When eight years old she found a volume of Shakespeare, and was so fascinated that she could hardly put the book down. It is said that her father advised her not to try by dress and orna-ments to attract, for her mind, not her face, was her attraction. She took the advice and studied until her knowledge astonished people, and her gift of talk added to her power. She held conversations like Al-cott, edited *The Dial*, was a literary critic, and wrote several essays. *Woman in the Nineteenth Century* is her strongest paper. Going over to Italy, she met and married an Italian, the Marquis Ossoli. On her return voyage to America she, her husband, and their baby boy were drowned off Fire Island.

Summary.—Awakening of New England, 1810–50. Religious movement culminating in Uni-tarianism, the question being agitated princi-pally from 1815 to 1832.

William Ellery Channing (1780–1842), leader of Unitarianism, lecturer, orator; *Milton* and *Self-Culture*, finest papers on literary subjects.

Theodore Parker (1810–60), Transcendentalist and abolitionist. Literary movement, Transcen-dentalism, beginning 1832. The time of new ideas and isms, 1830–40.

Three Concord Writers: Amos Bronson Alcott (1799–1888), *Concord Days, Tablets, Table Talk, Son-nets and Canzonets.* Henry David Thoreau

(1817–62), *Walden*, best work; *A Week on the Concord and Merrimac Rivers.* Margaret Fuller Ossoli (1810–50) wrote essays and literary criticisms; *Woman in the Nineteenth Century*, best paper.

Some Thoughts from Channing.

God be thanked for books. They are the voices of the distant and dead, and make us heirs of the spiritual life of past ages. Books are the true levelers. They give to all who will faithfully use them the society, the spiritual presence, of the best and greatest of our race. No matter how poor I am, though the prosperous of my own time will not enter my obscure dwelling, if the sacred writers will enter and take up their abode under my roof, if Milton will cross my threshold to sing to me of Paradise, and Shakespeare to open to me the worlds of imagination and the workings of the human heart, and Franklin to enrich me with his practical wisdom, I shall not pine for want of intellectual companionship, and I may become a cultivated man though excluded from what is called the best society in the place where I live.

It is chiefly through books that we enjoy intercourse with superior minds, and these invaluable means of communication are in the reach of all. In the best books great men talk to us, give us their most precious thoughts, and pour their soul into ours.

SELF-CULTURE.

Thought, in its true sense, is an energy of intellect.

All virtue lies in individual action, in inward energy, in self-determination.

From Theodore Parker.

Every man has at times in his mind the Ideal of what he should be but is not. . . . Man never falls so low that he can see nothing higher than himself.

Yet, if he would, man cannot live all to this world. If not religious he will be superstitious. If he worship not the true God he will have his idols.

In this country every one gets a mouthful of education, but scarcely any one gets a full meal.

Every rose is an autograph from the hand of the Almighty God.

From Amos B. Alcott.

One cannot celebrate books sufficiently. After saying his best still something better remains to be spoken in their praise.

That is a good book which is opened with expectation and closed with profit.

The books that charmed us in youth recall the delight ever afterwards: we are hardly persuaded there are any like them, any deserving equally our affections.

The deepest truths are best read between the lines, and for the most part refuse to be written.

From Thoreau.

Public opinion is a weak tyrant compared with our own private opinion: what a man thinks of himself, that it is which determines, or rather indicates, his fate.

None are so old as those who have outlived enthusiasm.

Be not simply good — be good for something.

Read the best books first, or you may not have a chance to read them at all.

Nothing goes by luck in composition.

CHAPTER XIII.

RALPH WALDO EMERSON, THE "SAGE OF CONCORD."

America's Greatest Philosopher. — There is one name in the Transcendental list that stands for its best and deepest thought, and for America's best and deepest thought, for it is the name of one of the world's thinkers. It is that of Ralph Waldo Emerson, to whom hundreds looked up as disciples to a teacher and master, reminding us of Grecian days when men gathered around the sages and philosophers and were taught by them how to think and live. Emerson's father, grandfather, great-grandfather as far back as seven generations, had been preachers. The little boy inherited from these generations of pious men a refined, lovely nature that did not find it hard to do right. His home was such as would be expected — grave, dignified, religious, and literary. The child was taught high moral ideas, love of truth, patience, and self-control, and he inherited a love for books. His father was a man of literary tastes, and was vice-president of the Anthology Club, which founded the *North American Review*.

Emerson was born in Boston, May 25, 1803. His father dying eight years afterwards, the boy was trained by his mother, and by an aunt who was a fine classical scholar. The mother determined that her boys should be educated, and fought bravely with poverty. A letter to her eldest son, William, in answer to some complaints about his room and fare, reminds us of the ancient Spartan mothers: "Every-thing respecting you is doubtless interesting to me, but your domestic arrangements the least of anything, as these make no part of the man or character any further than he learns humility from his dependence on such trifles." No wonder Ralph Waldo Emerson cared so little for things money can buy! Like his mother, he considered luxuries "trifles;" he always lived simply and had few wants. At ten he was at-tending the Latin School, and at fourteen Harvard, being helped there by his brother William, who had earned the money by teaching—not enough money, however, to keep Ralph from being hampered by poverty.

Never caring for honors, he did not distinguish himself at school, had not a bit of talent for mathe-matics, and disliked the sciences too. But he loved literature and the languages, and read a great deal, especially poetry. Two old writers—Plato, the Greek philosopher who loved the beautiful so much and spoke so inspiringly of the soul, and Montaigne, a French essayist—are the ones to whom he owed the most. Shakespeare and Plutarch were two other favorites. The works of these four carefully read cannot make Emersons of all of us, but they will help to make intelligent people of those who study them. After he was graduated he taught school, and began to study for the ministry with Channing, whose influence over him was great. His health breaking down, he went to Florida, still teaching school during the intervening winters until 1829, when he became colleague of the pastor of the Second Unitarian Church in Boston. That same year he married, but lost his wife a few months afterwards. He did not believe all the doctrines of the church, and finally gave up the ministry altogether.

Men like Allston and Channing had roused a desire for culture, had made Americans acquainted with German and German writers, had brought to us the new thoughts that were astir in Europe. One man particularly enthusiastic over German, Edward Everett, distinguished as a teacher and as an orator, had much to do with shaping Emerson's mind. Other great men of the time influenced him. Going to England, he met three famous writers—Wordsworth, Coleridge, and Carlyle: Wordsworth the poet of Nature and simplicity; Coleridge the poet, philosopher, and devoted German student; Carlyle the essayist and moralist, also filled with German ideas. Emerson's friendship with Carlyle was never broken, and he introduced to us Carlyle's books. Carlyle was very bitter towards most of the world, and few were not mocked by his bitter pen; but of Emerson he says: "One of the most lovable creatures in himself we had ever looked upon." All that ever knew him say the same.

Lecturer and Poet. — For forty-six years Emerson lived and lectured at Concord. He made the lecture platform what it is to-day, for he was the first real lecturer. These lectures, polished and changed somewhat to suit a different form, make up his essays, for in literature it is as an essayist, poet, and philosopher that he has his high place. His first famous verses, *The Concord Hymn*, he read April 19, 1836, at the anniversary of the battle of Lexington. Two lines in it are almost as famous as the event which they celebrate:

> " Here once the embattled farmers stood,
>   And fired the shot heard round the world."

"Nature."—The same year appeared his first book, *Nature*, full of the most beautiful descriptions of

Nature, which he profoundly and thoroughly understood and exulted in.   He stood rapt before the
works of Nature; he joyed in a morning walk even
through slush and cold.   But he insists that Nature
is given simply to teach our minds, and that the laws
which govern the outside objects of Nature are just
the same as those that govern our souls.   So this
book is not entirely about outdoors.   He discusses
the same deep subjects which Jonathan Edwards did,
but arrives at very different conclusions.   These conclusions are called his philosophy,—the Emersonian
philosophy,—and he tells his views again and again
in his poetry and essays.   Jonathan Edwards believed
we were born with bad tempers, and that it was far
easier to do wrong than to do right.   Emerson believed everybody had at birth a chance to start right as
Adam had or an angel might have; and if a man
can "command Nature, God shows Himself anew in
him."   Emerson, you see, judged others by himself.
His disposition was a very remarkable one, for he
lived a serene, pure life, apparently untroubled by the
wicked feelings with which most people have to con-
tend.   His conscience did not hurt him; he did not
have to go through shame and repentance for "being wicked;" and he had but few temptations in his
placid life.   Thus he lived calmly, modestly, and gen-
erously, unconsciously setting before admiring eyes
the example of an ideal man.   Yet when they asked
from his lips how he overcame sin and temptation,
they got no rules by which they could "do the example."   Only one Teacher has ever taken His disciples' hearts and changed them from bad to good;
only one Book lays down the rules for holiness so
plainly that we can follow them and reach the life
we wish to reach.

When Emerson tries to explain his philosophy

or to reason about it, it is hard to understand him. The story is that when asked to explain one of his difficult sayings he acknowledged that he did not know what he had meant, but that he felt that way when he wrote it. He looked into his own soul for the visions he saw, and told of these visions, believing that every man could see and feel as he did. Though this was a mistake, there is many a helpful bit of advice in his writings which we can follow, and even young people will enjoy much that he has said. Those who wish can always skip the parts that are mystical, for his short sentences are like separate sayings.

His Influence.— His influence is especially beneficial to young men and young women. He makes them think, and think for themselves, putting in them high hopes and high aims. He had the brains that waken up other brains and set them in motion; and perhaps no other human being has ever done so much to " elevate the purpose," and to make men see that getting money, spending money, seeking success in buying farms, cattle, and furniture, is a low aim unworthy of their endeavors. " Hitch your wagon to a star," was his idea. Not rich himself, he always had money to give, away, and he thus writes in his journal : " Rich, say you ? How rich ? Rich enough to help anybody, rich enough to succor the friendless, the unfashionable, the eccentric." The aims he puts before us are humility, sincerity, obedience, submission, and longings to grow grander in soul. Read all you find by him on books and literature. His lectures were some of them biographical, being on Milton, Carlyle, and others ; some were on English literature, history, human life, human culture, and the times. His oration before the Phi Beta Kappa Society on *Man Thinking, or the American Scholar*, had an extraordinary effect. The aisles were crowded and breathless, the windows filled with eager heads. It made him the leader of New England in literary matters. His house was like a famous shrine, for men and women flocked there, and sat down before him to learn from him.

His Manners.—To the queer, eccentric, even disagreeable people that crowded around him he was exquisitely polite and gentle, lending a helping hand and listening to their wild schemes, though he himself was practical and full of common sense—"a Greek head on right Yankee shoulders." His boast was, "Any man that knocks at my door shall have my attention." To college boy or schoolgirl he was always ready, not only to talk, but to listen. The students to whom he lectured reverenced him. One has told us of "the old, quiet, modest gentleman" who sat down by him and chatted of "college matters," of "books and reading," always as if he "expected as much as he gained." He was devoted to children—entertained all in Concord once a year. Even the babies smiled at him, cooed at him, and loved him. In everything and everybody he saw only the good and beautiful, never the bad and ugly.

His Books.—Though one of the founders of American literature, his books are neither many nor large. They consist of his poems and short essays. Some of these essays are on such subjects as "Self-Reliance," "Manners," "Behavior," "Love," "Friendship," "Character." His way of writing was to jot down in little notebooks any thoughts that came to him; then, working in his study every morning, he very slowly put these thoughts together, spending days, months, and even years sometimes, before he was satisfied with one essay. Each sentence is generally so short and so to the point that it can be quoted like a proverb.

His poetry can be quoted too, for it is like his prose,—it says something; it is high and deep, most of it, but the youngest child can enjoy his little piece, *The Mountain and the Squirrel.* The mountain and the squirrel had a quarrel, and when the mountain called the squirrel "little prig," the squirrel replied that, though not "very big," nor able to carry trees on its back, there were two things it could do that the mountain could not do : the mountain could not crack a nut nor climb a tree. One of the poems is on a *Humblebee*, another on a *Chickadee*, another on a *Snow-storm ;* for Emerson so loved country life and country sights that on his walks a bird or a flower would suggest lovely thoughts and words.

I have told you so much about the man and his life, more than about his writings, because it was the man and his life that gave him such a wonderful influence, that caused others to declare with pride, " I am Emersonian in my creed," illustrating the truth of Emerson's own lines :

> " Nor knowest thou what argument
> Thy life to thy neighbor's creed hath lent."

Seeing his life, they thought it was made by his creed or beliefs ; but it was his life that made his creed. He died in his eightieth year, in 1882.

Summary. — RALPH WALDO EMERSON (1803–82), lecturer, poet, essayist, and philosopher. Born in Boston, of a long line of ministers ; lived at Concord. Leader of the Transcendentalists, a great thinker, and of unequaled influence on other minds.
Essays on Literary and Moral Subjects : Nature his first book. *Self-Reliance, History*, and *Friendship*,

some essays in first series; *Character, Manners,*
in second series.

*Other Volumes of Lectures or Essays: Representative
Men, Conduct of Life, Society and Solitude, Letters and Social Aims.*

*Poems: Each and All, The Sphinx, The Problem,
Wood-notes, May-day, The Snow-storm, The
Humblebee, The Chickadee, Concord Hymn, The
Rhodora, The Days.*

Well-known Words from Emerson.

Every rational creature has all Nature for his dowry
and estate.   It is his if he will.   He may divest himself
of it; he may creep into a corner and abdicate his kingdom, as most men do; but he is entitled to the world
by his constitution.   In proportion to the energy of his
thought and will he takes up the world into himself.

Nature stretcheth out her arms to embrace man: only
let his thoughts be of equal greatness.

The silence that accepts merit as the most natural thing
in the world is the highest applause.

An innavigable sea washes with silent waves between
us and the things we aim at and converse with.

Life is a train of moods like a string of beads, and as
we pass through them they prove to be the many-colored
lenses which paint the world their own hue.

Character is the centrality, the impossibility of being
displaced or overset.

No circumstances can repair a defect in character.

—Self-trust is the essence of heroism.

The hearing ear is always found close to the speaking
tongue.

Trust men, and they will be true to you; treat them
greatly, and they will show themselves great.

His heart was as great as the world, but there was no
room in it to hold the memory of a wrong.

The highest compact we can make with our fellow is :
let there be truth between us two forevermore. . . . It

is sublime to feel and say of another, I need never meet or speak or write to him; we need not reïnforce ourselves, or send tokens of remembrance: I rely on him as on myself.

—The days are made on a loom whereof the warp and woof are past and future time.

Write it on your heart that every day is the best day in the year. No man has learned anything rightly until he knows that every day is doomsday.

—Good manners are made up of petty sacrifices.

The most interesting writing is that which does not quite satisfy the reader. . . . The trouble with most writers is, they spread too thin.

Take it for granted that truths will harmonize; and as for the falsities and mistakes, they will speedily die of themselves.

Out of your own self should come your theme, and only thus can your genius be your friend.

—Don't run after ideas. Save and nourish them, and you will have all you should entertain. They will come close enough and keep you busy.

Do not attempt to be a great reader; and read for facts, and not by the bookful.

Life is not so short but there is always time for courtesy.

Genius unexerted is no more genius than a bushel of acorns is a forest of oaks. There may be epics in men's brains just as there are oaks in acorns; but the tree and book must come out before we can measure them. . . . How many men would fain go to bed dunces and wake up Solomons! . . . Those who sow dunce seed, vice seed, laziness seed, usually get a crop. . . . A man of mere capacity undeveloped is only an organized daydream with a skin on it. . . . A flint and a genius that will not strike fire are no better than wet junkwood.

—Truth is the summit of being; justice is the application of it to affairs.

The world is his who can see through its pretensions. . . . The day is always his who works in it with serenity and great aims.

—Knowledge is the knowing that we cannot know. Our knowledge is the amassed thought and experience of innumerable minds.

Light is the first of painters. There is no object so foul that intense light will not make it beautiful.

All writing comes by the grace of God, and all doing and having.

> If eyes were made for seeing,
> Then beauty is its own excuse for being.
>   THE RHODORA.

> Wiser far than human seer,
> Yellow-breeched philosopher;
> Seeing only what is fair,
> Sipping only what is sweet,
> Thou dost mock at fate and care,
> Leave the chaff and take the wheat.
>   TO THE HUMBLEBEE.

> And ye shall succor men ;
>   'Tis nobleness to serve ;
> Help them who cannot help again ;
>   Beware from right to swerve.
>   BOSTON HYMN.

> Deep in the man sits fast his fate, . . .
> To mold his fortunes mean or great :
> Unknown to Cromwell as to me
> Was Cromwell's measure or degree.
>   FATE.

> Only to children children sing,
> Only to youth will spring be spring.
>   THE HARP.

> When half-gods go
> The gods arrive.

> Mount to paradise
> By the stairway of surprises.

> What is excellent,
> As God lives, is permanent.

CHAPTER XIV.

Orators and Statesmen, and Political Parties.
—It is only because so much writing has been done
about the important public questions of the day that
the names of the orators and statesmen of America
must be mentioned at all in this work. Just like newspapers, however, this kind of writing, though mighty
in its influence at the time, loses much of its interest
when the question has become a dead issue and the
contest has been settled one way or the other. Long,
long before the war was thought of, when Washington, Hamilton, and Jefferson were yet alive, there
were two parties, as you remember, one saying that
the Union was just a voluntary agreement, and that
any State could withdraw if she thought there was
good reason; the other denying this, and giving more
power to the government at Washington. Disputes
arose very often between the two parties, getting more
and more bitter as the question of slavery came to
the front.

The Slavery Question. — The negroes not suiting
the North, and its colder climate not suiting them,
the slaves were all in the South, where the rich plant-
ers who owned them lived on immense plantations
worked by these slaves. Negroes were the chief
property of the region, and nobody thought at first
of their being freed. But it was proposed that slavery

should not be allowed in the new States admitted into the Union. The South objected that such a regulation would be against the Constitution, and as each new State was added there were hot disputes in Congress and many fierce wrangles. Two men in the Senate, Daniel Webster and Henry Clay, saved the Union by the compromises which their efforts brought about.

Webster and Clay. — In many respects these two orators can be described together. Both were poor boys, Webster in his New Hampshire home, Clay in his Virginia one. Webster's wise father saw his son's superiority, and with great self-denial sent him to school; and the young man continued the struggle and obtained a college education. Henry Clay's father, a Baptist preacher, died and left his family very, very poor. Often the barefooted boy, dressed in a hickory shirt and cotton pantaloons held up by a single suspender, would plow all day, or would be seen taking a bag of corn to mill, riding bareback. One of his pet names was "The Mill-boy of the Slashes," the section from which he came being called "The Slashes" of Hanover County, Virginia. Both boys practiced speaking to the horses and cows, both won laurels in their youth, both soon became prominent public men, were sent to Congress, held the office of Secretary of State, and both were disappointed as they seemed ready to grasp the highest prize, the Presidency of the United States. Both died in 1852. Side by side they worked in the cause of peace, Webster representing Massachusetts, his adopted State, a State so strongly antislavery that her people could not forgive him for his more moderate views; Clay representing his adopted State, Kentucky, a slave-holding State, a State that has ever regarded his name as her brightest ornament. Webster, however, has a far higher place in literature. Clay's power was in his personal magnetism, in his ability to win and manage people. He made no attempt to be a writer. One sentence of his should be engraved in the memory, heart, and life of every young man : " I had rather be right than be President." So great were his services in making peace between the two parties that he was known as " The Great Pacificator."

Daniel Webster's Orations were not all made on political subjects. Two of the grandest were delivered at the laying of the cornerstone of Bunker Hill monument and at the completion of the monument. Famous is his speech in a murder case, a speech in which a murderer's tortured conscience is so eloquently described. Famous also is his eulogy on Adams and Jefferson. Everything—voice, appearance, and genius—combined to make him an orator. So striking was his appearance that the coal-heavers on the streets of Liverpool stopped to stare at him when he passed them. His massive head was like a Greek god's. So impressive was the roll of his thunderous voice that he could utter strings of meaningless sentences and thereby move his listeners.

One idea ruled Webster's life, and it is found in that powerful reply to the Southern orator, Robert Y. Hayne, and in these words: " Liberty and Union, now and forever, one and inseparable." Nobody else did so much to preserve the Union. Yet after all he had done, after all the honors he had gained, he died a saddened man, the people of his own State having turned against him on account of his stand on the Fugitive Slave Law. Not until years later did the cloud lift that had blotted out of view his truthfulness of purpose and the consistency of his conduct.

John C. Calhoun.— Always linked with the names of Webster and Clay is a third name, John C. Calhoun, another " giant " in the Senate in brains and

power.   He was as unswerving an upholder of States'
rights as Webster was of the Union.   A deep thinker
and reasoner, he made clear, concise, logical speeches,
and could be most convincing.   His own State, South
Carolina, obeyed his advice absolutely.   No enemy
could bring any charge against his perfect upright-
ness of character.   He knew no trick of the politician or of the pleasing speaker.   He was a statesman first, then an orator.

Edward Everett. — Our most polished, elegant
orator during this period was a man who did much for
culture in our country — Edward Everett, a statesman,
lecturer, poet, preacher, teacher.   He edited the *North
American Review*, writing fifty of its articles; was
president of Harvard; served in Congress; was Secretary of State, minister to England, and candidate
for the office of Vice-President.   Yet notwithstanding his brilliant career he did not make for himself
" an ever-to-be-remembered name" in literature.   His
eulogy on Webster, and an oration on *Circumstances
Favorable to the Progress of Literature in America*,
are very fine.   Especially beautiful in the latter oration
is an apostrophe to Lafayette, who was a guest of
the Phi Beta Kappa Society of Harvard, the society
before whom the oration was made.

Abolitionist Orators. — Next to Webster as an
orator was Wendell Phillips, the great champion of
the abolitionists, whose speeches against slavery rang
like the trumpet calling to battle.   His best strength
belonged to the antislavery cause ; but after the struggle was over he turned aside to think and speak on other
topics, making literary addresses that are eloquent.   On
New-Year's day, 1831, William Lloyd Garrison had
founded a paper, *The Liberator*, whose sole object
was to abolish, or put an end to, slavery.   For thirty-
five years he edited this paper, in the mean while form-

ing societies for the same object, speaking, writing, working with this end before him. He cared nothing for the political idea; his one idea was that slavery was a most awful crime, and that, Constitution or no Constitution, it ought to be stamped out. He was the leader of the abolitionists. Now that slavery is done away with, it is hard for us to realize that the abolitionists were hated, abused, maltreated, not only at the South, but in the North. It was through the streets of Boston that Garrison was dragged by a rope tied round his body. It was this sight which made Wendell Phillips determine to espouse the cause. There were fanatics in the party, people who could see only one side, and they roused hatred by their violence. Four years of awful bloodshed, and the abolition of slavery was the outcome. The strongest abolitionist statesman was Charles Sumner. He was a most influential speaker, *The True Grandeur of Nations* being one of his well-known orations.

Summary.—Daniel Webster (1782–1852), born in New Hampshire; our grandest orator.

Henry Clay (1777–1852), born in Virginia, Kentucky his home; orator.

John C. Calhoun (1782–1850), South Carolina; statesman.

Robert Y. Hayne (1791–1839), South Carolina; orator.

Edward Everett (1794–1865), Massachusetts; orator, preacher, teacher, and poet.

William Lloyd Garrison (1805–79), Massachusetts; abolitionist and editor of *The Liberator.*

Wendell Phillips (1811–84), Massachusetts; orator of abolitionists. Literary addresses fine.

Charles Sumner (1811–74), Massachusetts; statesman.

CHAPTER XV.

JOHN GREENLEAF WHITTIER, THE POET OF NEW ENGLAND.

The Quaker Poet. — It is impossible to speak of the days when the question of slavery agitated the country without recalling Whittier, sometimes called " The Laureate of the Abolitionists." He has several other endearing titles — "The Quaker Poet," " The Hebrew Poet," " The Prophet Bard," — but the one name most descriptive of him is " The Poet of New England." It is of New England traditions, of the life, homes, and people of New England, that he writes, and in his poems he gives voice to the feelings and opinions of New England people. John G. Whittier was born Dec. 17, 1807, near Haverhill, Massachusetts, a village nestled in the Merrimac valley. We know well the little farmhouse and its inmates: the father, "a prompt, decisive man," who never wasted breath in words; the mother turning her spinning wheel, telling "the story of her early days;" the "uncle innocent of books," but "rich in love of fields and brooks," "a simple, guileless, childlike man;" the unmarried aunt, "a calm and gracious element," "welcome wheresoe'er she went;" the elder sister, "truthful and almost sternly just, impulsive, earnest, prompt to act;" the "youngest and dearest" with her "large, sweet, asking eyes;" and even the schoolmaster, "brisk wielder of the birch and rule:" for Whittier has in his *Snow-bound* faithfully pictured the members of the household.

"**Snow-bound.**"—In the same poem we learn how he and his brother did the nightly chores; of the gathering round the great fire when the work was done. We can see the apples sputtering in a row, and the basket of nuts provided to help them pass the long yet pleasant hours, "sped with stories old," " with puzzles wrought and riddles told ; " and when at nine o'clock the circle broke up we think of the light-hearted boys enjoying the voice of the wind that "round the gables roared," and careless of the "light-sifted " snowflakes that fell through the "un-plastered wall." It would seem a dreadful hardship now to be snow-bound a week in a poor little country home ; but though they had to "read and re-read their little store " of books, and heard from the outside world only through the little village newspaper, Whittier had naught but sweetest memories of his boyhood, even in these shut-in times of snowy winter. When he speaks of himself as a barefoot boy he forgets everything except the delights of the country boy's life :

> "I was rich in flowers and trees,
>   Humming birds and honey bees ;
> For my sport the squirrel played,
>   Plied the snouted mole his spade"—

and in line after line he recalls the "outward sunshine, inward joy " "waiting on the barefoot boy." He made use of his eyes when a boy to learn "how the robin feeds her young," "where the whitest lilies blow," "where the ground nut trails its vine ; " for "Nature answered all he asked " as "hand in hand with her he walked," as "face to face with her he talked." These happy days were always fresh in his memory, and make his poetry fresh and natural.

Yet there was poverty, real poverty, and hard

work in his youth.   In the summer he helped to har-
vest, in the fall and spring to plow and sow, in the
winter to make shoes, — the shoemaker's bench was a
common sight in the New England houses.   There
was no money to pay for his schooling.   In his
Songs of Labor he has made labor more beautiful,
and probably speaks from experience when he hopes
these *Songs* will make the toilers "feel that life is
wisest spent"

"Where the strong working hand makes the strong
    working brain."

It was a sturdy, gracious home, with a Quaker calm
ever resting upon it.   Two books formed the library
of his childhood — the Bible and *Pilgrim's Progress.*
The Bible his mother explained to him as he stood
by her knee, and its influence is seen in all he wrote,
giving strength and point to his style.   No poetry came
in his way in his earliest years, for the one book they
had that was called "poetry" deserved not the name.
He was a lad in his teens when another book fell into
his hands and made him a poet.   An old friend of
his father's passing by stopped for the night.   In his
saddlebags he had two little volumes which he drew
forth, saying to John, "I have something to show
thee.   I think thee will like the book."   Those little
volumes were to Whittier what that first copy of
Wordsworth was to Bryant — "a revelation of what
poetry may be and do;" and they were written by one
far poorer than he, — Robert Burns, — and the poems
were on subjects he could understand, on such simple
things as the turning up of a mouse's nest or a daisy
with the plowshare.   That night Whittier read until
his mother sent him to bed.   Getting up at daylight
he was reading again, but the old gentleman kindly

said, "Thee likes the book, John: thee may keep it till I come back this way."

Whittier's first printed poem was in imitation of Burns, and we can imagine his feelings as he opened the paper, tossed by a neighbor into the field where the youth was at work, and saw his poem in print.　In all his after years there never came the same thrill again, though fame was his, and his name could be seen in scores of periodicals.　The paper was Garrison's *Free Press*.　Garrison recognized the talents of this new contributor, and went out to see him, finding him at the plow.　It was Garrison who strengthened Whittier's ambition to obtain an education.　With a little money made by shoemaking, our young poet when twenty years old attended the Haverhill Academy six months.　A session of school teaching enabled him to attend a few more months. A library belonging to a gentleman in Haverhill completed his course of education as far as quiet, leisurely study was concerned, for he became an editor.　He was first on one paper, then another, going from Boston to Haverhill, from Haverhill to Hartford, publishing in the mean while frequent poems and sketches. These were collected in his first book, *Legends of New England.*　He had loved to listen to the tales told by the fireside, and now he retold these tales in prose and verse.　Though his verses were not polished, they were liked.　Fame and favor were in his grasp, but he heard a call that to him seemed a call from God.

He gave up his literary ambitions to obey the call, to throw himself into the antislavery crusade. He joined Garrison on his newly established abolition paper, *The Liberator.*　He was made secretary of the Anti-Slavery Society.　He was ever ready with poem or pamphlet to serve the cause.　He "coolly faced" the mob that tore up the press of the *Pennsylvania Freeman*, which he was editing, and he would just as coolly have died for his beliefs. Narrowed by his past limitations, he saw only one side of slavery, the awful side. To him it was a crime, and nothing but a crime, to be wiped out at any cost, and, Quaker though he was, he cheered the Union soldiers with song and ballad. His poems against slavery were like the Psalms in their zeal, and they were trumpet calls to men to send them into battle. He accomplished his purpose; but his *Voices of Freedom* has lost much of its interest, as many of the poems were on passing events, and were often written hurriedly and carelessly. Doing editorial work on the *National Era* of Washington for twelve years, having to do with other periodicals, — with the *Atlantic Monthly*, for instance — he never lacked time to speak for the cause he loved. It was impossible for him to do his literary talents justice with so many other duties on hand. His poem on Webster entitled *Ichabod*, a lament over Webster's course on the Fugitive Slave Law, and *Barbara Frietchie*, founded on a newspaper incident of the war, are still quoted and recited. Yet we can no longer believe that Webster was

> " So fallen ! so lost ! the light withdrawn
> Which once he wore !
> The glory from his gray hairs gone
> Forevermore ! "

and we know there is no truth in the incident about Barbara Frietchie. *In War Time* and *National Lyrics* are on the same one theme.

Other favorite subjects with Whittier are old Colonial times in New England, and peaceful country home scenes in the same section. No other poet tells a story better, nor has any other described the quiet rural life so charmingly and so truthfully. *Mogg Megone* is a tale of Indian and Colonial life; *Cassandra Southwick*, of Quaker persecutions; *Mabel Martin*, of the days when witches were believed to exist. *Supernaturalism in New England* and *Margaret Smith's Journal* are prose tales on the same kind of topics. *Maud Muller*, so well known to everybody, and *The Barefoot Boy* are perfect gems of country scenes. Whittier wrote for children and about children; his loveliest poem, *Snow-bound*, was for *Our Young Folks*, a juvenile paper, and so was *In School-days*. It is in the latter we see the little maiden lingering to apologize for having "trapped" a boy in the spelling class:

> " ' I'm sorry that I spelled the word;
>   I hate to go above you,
>   Because,' the brown eyes lower fell,
>   ' Because, you see, I love you.' "

After the war his life was most serene, his best poetical work being done in his later years. His sister Elizabeth, and afterwards his niece, kept house for him, for he was never married. He touches so tenderly, so playfully, so truly on love, as in *Amy Wentworth* and *Among the Hills*, that we are sure he knew its spell. *My Playmate* and *Telling the Bees* may be glimpses into a *real* past, and it may have been that memories of the "playmate" kept him from marrying. His last years were spent at Danvers, Massachusetts, and his home, "Oak Knoll," was the resort of many of our most distinguished men. As he neither acquired a thorough education nor was broadened by travel, it is true of Whittier, as Lowell writes, that

" His grammar's not always correct, nor his rhymes,
  And he's prone to repeat his own lyrics sometimes."

But he can stir the blood, speak to the heart, and
help one to goodness and sincerity. In all the poems
that came from his pen there is a moral, in nearly
all there is religion, many being hymns. He said of
himself that he sat on his own doorstep and wrote
of what he saw from there; and in his *Proem*, a
preface to some of his poems, he speaks of

" The rigor of a frozen clime,
  The harshness of an untaught ear."

Though we may agree with him that

" Of mystic beauty, dreamy grace,
  No rounded art the lack supplies,"

we cannot agree with him in the line about Nature:

" I view her common forms with unanointed eyes."

He views her "common forms," but it is with the
poet's heavenly anointed eyes.

Honors were heaped upon him on his seventieth
and eightieth birthdays. Other great poets dedicated
poems to him, poems full of love and admiration.
Each birthday of his latter years was an ovation of
letters, messages, telegrams, and gifts of congratula-
tion. His own last poem was a birthday offering to
Oliver Wendell Holmes. He died in 1892, mourned
by the whole country.

Summary.—JOHN GREENLEAF WHITTIER (1807–
    92), Massachusetts, our great ballad poet and
    the poet of abolition.
Poems: Against slavery: *Voices of Freedom, In War
    Time.* Of New England, *Legends of New Eng-
    land, Snow-bound,* and many others. *Songs of*

Labor. The Tent on the Beach. Short, well-known
poems : *Maud Muller, The Barefoot Boy, Among
the Hills, My Playmate,* etc.   *Cassandra Southwick, Barclay of Ury, Mabel Martin, Skipper
Ireson's Ride, In School-days, Ichabod,* and *Barbara Frietchie.*
Prose : Leaves from Margaret Smith's Journal.

Lines from Whittier that Everybody Knows.

> For of all sad words of tongue or pen,
> The saddest are these : " It might have been."
> Ah, well ! for us all some sweet hope lies
> Deeply buried from human eyes ;
> And in the hereafter, angels may
> Roll the stone from the grave away.
> MAUD MULLER.

> Oh, rank is good, and gold is fair,
>   And high and low mate ill ;
> But love has never known a law
>   Beyond its own sweet *will.*
> AMY WENTWORTH.

> Happy he whose inward ear,
> Angel comfortings can hear,
> O'er the rabble's laughter.
> BARCLAY OF URY.

> Easier to smite with Peter's sword,
>   Than watch one hour in humbling prayer ;
> Life's " great things," like the Syrian lord,
>   Our hearts can do and dare.
> THE CYPRESS TREE OF CEYLON.

> The tissue of the life to be
>   We weave with colors all our own,
> And in the field of Destiny,
>   We reap as we have sown.
> RAPHAEL.

> When faith is lost, when honor dies,
> The man is dead !
> ICHABOD.

CHAPTER XVI

MEN WHO HAVE WRITTEN HISTORY.

Qualifications of an Historian. — Although history is one of the most important divisions of literature, yet no great history was written in our country until after 1830. This is not strange, however, when we think what is required to write a real history, one that tells how and why events have come to pass. An historian needs a stupendous amount of patience, perseverance, and capacity for hard labor. He must look over files of old papers, study up dry, dusty documents, and search and search that he may find out accurately every fact. He must possess a trained mind and memory, judgment to know what is important, imagination to make the facts entertaining; in short, he must have almost every gift belonging to any great writer. He must have a large library and abundant leisure, for it may require many years to complete his history; and it is well for him to travel and to learn other languages. All these things mean that he must be a man of property — and not many writers are rich. Fortunately for us, there have appeared just such historians. Three great ones who attained fame before the war are Prescott, Motley, and Bancroft, all natives of Massachusetts and graduates of Harvard. Motley and Bancroft both held high offices under the government as ministers to foreign lands, and Prescott had every advantage of foreign travel.

William Hickling Prescott was born in 1796 at

Salem, Massachusetts, his father being a distinguished lawyer, his grandfather the Prescott of the Revolutionary War who fortified Breed's Hill. The family moving to Boston, he spent his boyhood there. He went to Harvard at fifteen, having made up his mind to be a lawyer. An accident put an end to this hope, for while he and his classmates were having a "jolly time" at a class dinner one of the boys playfully threw a bread crust across the table at Prescott, completely destroying the sight of one eye. The other eye became affected through sympathy. For six weeks the young man was confined in a totally dark room with absolutely nothing to amuse him but his own thoughts. These must have been brave, sunny thoughts, however, for instead of giving up all ambition on account of his blindness, it was made stronger than before. For two years he traveled in England, France, and Italy, consulting all the great oculists; but none could help him, and he returned, married, and bent himself to the task of writing the *History of Ferdinand and Isabella*, the King and Queen of Spain. In spite of his infirmity, Prescott mastered the languages and literature of Europe, and when his sight failed again he employed a reader — one ignorant of Spanish — to read the old Spanish histories and other records to him. His habit was to listen several hours to this reading, then walk five miles to think over it, and finally by dictating, or by means of a little instrument suited to blind people, he would daily write fifty or sixty pages from memory. He was more than ten years on his *Ferdinand and Isabella*, and, after all this time and labor had been spent, hesitated about publishing it, so unusual was his modesty. A few copies having been struck off, friends persuaded him to publish it, and it was immediately successful, not only here, but in Spain, Germany, and

France, for it was translated into the languages of those countries. The laborious preparation of those ten years made it far easier for him to write two other histories, *The Conquest of Mexico* and *The Conquest of Peru.* He was writing still another, *The History of Philip II.*, when paralysis came upon him, and he passed away in 1859, honored here and abroad. His histories are the highest authority on the period they cover, and there is a charm in his style that makes the driest facts interesting. In his blindness he must have made pictures to himself of the scenes during those exciting years when Ferdinand and Isabella reigned, and of the romantic incidents connected with Cortez and Pizarro, the cruel Spaniards who conquered Mexico and Peru; for he writes so vividly that his readers seem to see the wild and dreadful scenes which he describes.

John Lothrop Motley was born at Dorchester, Massachusetts, in 1814. He showed a remarkable brightness when only a small boy. At ten he speaks in his letters of a novel he was reading as being "better than any new novel I have read for two or three years except Scott's," and says of a French history: "I think it very interesting, and it is much more so by its being in French." These expressions sound quite old and book-loving from such a young boy, and so do his requests written from his school for "books, books, and newspapers; nothing to eat and nothing to drink — but books." He was sent to Mr. Bancroft's school, Round Hill Academy; then to Harvard College, where he was graduated when barely seventeen. His intense love of knowledge was still as strong as when he had begged for books, and going to Germany he studied law and became thoroughly at home in the modern languages. Most young men possessed of his many gifts would have been tempted to neglect learning; for Motley was received into the best society, and he was one of the handsomest of men, a perfect type of the Spanish face. The charms of society did not charm him from studying, but he was thirty years old before he determined to be a writer. He first tried his hand on two novels, both unsuccessful; then spent six months in Russia as an official member of legation; and finally made up his mind to write a history of Holland's heroic resistance to Spain in the sixteenth century.

His First Historical Work.—There was not enough material in the United States to furnish the data for such a work. He accordingly went to Holland, there to hunt through mountains of papers to find one little truth, having to learn new languages before he could read some of them, even to discover the key to ciphers of old secret state documents. He used to say that he did not know the living people of Holland, but if he could wake up in the sixteenth century he would be on intimate terms with every prominent Dutchman he would meet. It took ten years of this weary toil to prepare *The Rise of the Dutch Republic*, but the reward it brought him was worth twice ten years. Europe as well as America read and praised it. Though in three large volumes, not a page or a line is tedious. More fascinating than any story, you cannot lay it down until it is finished. You see the people in it; your blood boils with indignation over the horrible cruelties of the Spanish; you are filled with enthusiasm for the pluckiness of little Holland; and her leader, William the Silent, is loved like Washington, of whom he reminds you. Everybody in the book becomes your friend or your enemy, for the historian's characters live before you.

Motley's other two histories of *The United Netherlands* and *John of Barneveld* continue the

story of the Dutch.   From 1858 for twelve years
Motley found nothing but honors awaiting him.   Oxford University in England conferred on him the title
of D.C.L., the Queen of Holland sought his acquaintance, and for six years he was our minister to Austria.
Yet his last seven years were not joyful.   His feelings were deeply hurt because he was recalled when
minister to England, — a change due to some political
trick, — and he describes himself as " ill, weary, and
overworked."   He died in Dorchester, England, in
1877.

George Bancroft. — Prescott and Motley wrote on
foreign countries ; George Bancroft, on our own.   Born
in the closing year of the eighteenth century, he lingered
nearly through the nineteenth, until 1891, even then a
hale, hearty old man in full possession of his senses.   We
know partly the secret of his strong health.   His family
had for generations led simple lives, frugal in their
habits, thinking high rather than living high ; and Bancroft in the midst of his heaviest work "never forgot
to take plenty of sleep, and a long gallop daily," and
he never worried.   Going to school when he was little required a daily four-mile walk ; but at eleven he
was sent to Exeter Academy, to one of America's
best schoolmasters, Dr. Abbott.   At thirteen he was
ready for Harvard.   Edward Everett, his tutor in
Greek, suggested in a letter that a young man be
chosen to prepare for the next vacant professorship :
Bancroft was the one sent.   He was in Europe five
years, studying diligently several languages, German
literature and Greek philosophy, but especially history.
He made a tour through part of the Continent on foot,
meeting all the most famous men.   To please his
father he was licensed to preach, but, though Jonathan Edwards's writings had made him a very strong
believer in the doctrines of his own church, his heart

was more in literature than in preaching. He turned aside first to be professor at Harvard, then to found Round Hill Academy, where he taught ten years. He was active in politics as a Democrat, though to please his wife he refused several offices to which he was chosen. He did finally accept a place, first as collector of the port (he procured Hawthorne's appointment at Salem), then as Secretary of the Navy, and as minister successively to England, to Russia, and to Berlin, filling each position well. It is to him we owe the Naval Academy at Annapolis.

Bancroft's Great Work. — His public official services, however, are not his chief glory. His *History of the United States* is his lifework, for it was fifty years between the first and the last volume. It required a great deal of patient toiling, and it met with great success, not only here and in Europe, but also in South America, where it was introduced that it might awaken there the love of liberty. These ten or twelve great volumes bring the history only to 1789, through the adoption of the Constitution. Probably no other man will try to write up that period so fully again, but many smaller histories will be made from Bancroft's. It is clear and accurate, but too long for busy people to use except — as they do a dictionary — as a reference book. Bancroft's winter home was in Washington, his summer home in Newport, and it was hard to tell which was most interesting to see, his library of 12,000 works overflowing floor and window seats, or his beautiful rose garden, for he loved roses as he loved books.

Francis Parkman. — Two years later than Bancroft, in 1893, died a remarkable historian, Francis Parkman, one who comes to the point in all his stories and is strong and brilliant. I say his "stories," for whoever loves to read of Indians, exciting adventures, and fighting will find them in his history. He chose for his subject the French in America : the days when Catholic missionaries tried to convert the Indians; the days when the French trappers lived on the Great Lakes; the days when the French, with their Indian allies, fought the English step by step for the supremacy in America. Before leaving Harvard he chose his subject, and, in order to know thoroughly the Indians, he went out to the far West in 1846, where he lived among the Indians, eating their poor food, sleeping in their dirty wigwams, joining them in their hunts, learning their ways and histories. His first volume, *The Oregon Trail*, tells of these experiences, experiences which nearly killed him then, injured his health permanently, and helped to bring on partial blindness. Upon his great history, *France and England in North America*, he spent fifty years, bringing it out in six or seven separate volumes, each distinct in itself; as, *La Salle, Montcalm and Wolfe, The Jesuits in North America*. He too was devoted to flowers, and was once professor of horticulture at Harvard. A new lily has been named after him.

Other Historians.—Others have taken their own land or portions of their own land as their theme. John Gorham Palfrey, in his *History of New England*, has shown us the Puritans. Hubert Howe Bancroft has done for the Pacific States what George Bancroft did for the whole country. Two professors, one of the Pennsylvania University,—John Bach McMaster,—one formerly of Harvard,—John Fiske,—have selected almost the same titles for their volumes: *History of the People of the United States* and *History of the American People*. Professor McMaster has prepared a delightful *Life of Benjamin Franklin*. Professor Fiske is known as a philosopher and an historical lecturer. Once he and some other literary people were talking of *Mother Goose*. He showed so much knowledge of the origin of its rhymes and jingles that he was invited by the editor of the *Atlantic Monthly*, who was present, to write the subject up: *Myths and Myth-makers* traces the history of many ancient legends, fairy stories, etc.

John Gilmary Shea has written on the same subjects as Parkman in *Discovery and Explorations of the Mississippi Valley*, *History of the Catholic Missions among the Indian Tribes*, and *History of New France*.

Several histories of the United States have appeared, there being one by Richard Hildreth in six volumes, one by Lossing, and *A Young Folks' History* of the same country by Higginson. Horace Scudder, another writer for children, has added a *History of the United States* to the half-dozen others on the same subject. Since the war there have been war papers by many of the chief actors in those exciting scenes, and several histories and memoirs of the great leaders. Jefferson Davis, for instance, has told us of the Confederacy, and General Grant has given us his *Memoirs*. But none of these writers would be called "historians."

Summary.—William Hickling Prescott (1796–1859), *History of Ferdinand and Isabella*, and histories of the conquests of Mexico and Peru— all on Spain and her conquests.

John Lothrop Motley (1814–77), *The Rise of the Dutch Republic*, *The History of the United Netherlands*, *The Life and Death of John of Barneveld* —all on Holland and its struggle for independence.

George Bancroft (1800–91), *History of the United States*, coming down to 1789, an immense work of twelve volumes.

Francis Parkman (1823–93), *France and England in North America*, seven volumes.

John Gorham Palfrey (1796–1881), *History of New England to* 1875, four volumes.

Benson J. Lossing (1813–92), historian and biographer.

John Gilmary Shea (1824–92), *New France, Catholic Missions among the Indians*, and many other volumes.

Richard Hildreth (1807–65), *History of the United States*, six volumes.

John Fiske (1842–   ), *History of the American People*. A philosopher as well as historian: *Myths and Myth-makers.*

John Bach McMaster (1852–   ), *Life of Benjamin Franklin, History of the People of the United States* (unfinished; it begins at 1789, and several volumes have appeared).

Thomas Wentworth Higginson (1823–   ), *Young Folks' History of the United States.*

Hubert Howe Bancroft (1832–   ), *History of the Pacific States*, forty volumes.

Horace E. Scudder (1838–   ), *History of the United States.* Writer also of books for children : *The Bodley Books.*

Gen. U. S. Grant (1822–85), *Personal Memoirs.*

Jefferson Davis (1808–89), *Rise and Fall of the Confederate Government.*

CHAPTER XVII.

OUR MOST WIDELY LOVED POET—H. W. LONGFELLOW.

Is there an American who is not acquainted with Longfellow? Surely you have heard of the midnight ride of Paul Revere; of the *Wreck of the Hesperus*, "the schooner that sailed the wintry sea;" of the youth who bore "a banner with the strange device, 'Excelsior!'" and of *The Children's Hour*, "between the dark and the daylight." I hope, too, that you have read how "through the forest walked Hiawatha;" how the schoolmaster pleaded for the "birds of Killingworth," "whose household words are songs in many keys;" and how the gentle Evangeline wandered through the "measureless prairies."

Childhood of Longfellow.—On the 27th of February, 1807, the same year with Whittier, was born Henry Wadsworth Longfellow in Portland, Maine, in "a great, square house by the sea," the first brick house ever built in the town. His father was a prominent lawyer; his mother had been a beautiful, lively young girl, who never lost her cheeriness though for years an invalid. All the advantages which Whittier lacked Longfellow had in his boyhood home. There was a good library into which he was turned loose to read. The first book that made a very distinct impression on him was Washington Irving's *Sketch-book*, published when he was about twelve or thirteen. This he read and re-read. From babyhood every opportunity in education was his, and he

109

made good use of his privileges. At three he started
to school to "Ma'am Fellows," as the children called
her; at six he composed his first letter; at seven he
was halfway through his Latin grammar. Always an
ambitious, studious boy, he loved best to lie under a
tree and read. He would tramp through the forest
with other lads, but the gun borne on his shoulder on
these occasions had little meaning, for in his grief
over the first bird he ever killed,—a robin redbreast,
—he resolved never to shoot another.

No one has written more lovingly of

> "The birds who make sweet music for us all
> In our dark days, as David did for Saul."

In *My Lost Youth* he speaks thus of his school-days:

> "I remember the gleams and gloams that dart
> Across the school-boy's brain;
> The song and the silence in the heart
> That in part are prophecies, and in part
> Are longings wild and vain."

His first printed poem, *The Battle of Lovell's
Pond,* came out in the Portland *Gazette* when he
was thirteen. The next year he entered Bowdoin
College, and during his four years there he published
twenty-four pieces of poetry and three prose sketches,
spending the money thus earned on a handsome copy
of *The Life of Chatterton*,[1] the boy poet of England. He must have felt unusual interest in Chatterton, for he chose him as the subject of his graduat-
ing essay; but his father advised some subject of
general interest. "Our Native Writers" was his
final choice. I wonder if he looked forward to the
day when no American could write or speak about

[1] Thomas Chatterton, a young poet of the eighteenth century who gave marks of unusual talent, but meeting with disappointment committed suicide when only seventeen.

our native writers and omit the name of Longfellow ?
He had a modest but clear knowledge of his own
talents, and had already written to his father of his
hope of becoming eminent some day.   He stood
high at college, so high that he could not write for his
final essay the class poem, as his classmates wished;
and he was loved by both professors and students.
He formed some lifelong friendships at Bowdoin.
But then no man, woman, or child could know the
sunny, genial, amiable, upright young man and not
love him.   Nor in the end did old age change him
for the worse.   The college authorities esteemed
him so highly that they elected him professor of
modern languages.   Gladly did he give up law,
which he disliked, to accept the position.   But he
first went to Europe to prepare, and there he remained three years, visiting France, Italy, Spain, and
Germany, and making himself thoroughly acquainted
with the language of each country.

Longfellow as Professor. — For five years he
taught at Bowdoin, doing his work very enthusiastically.   The Spanish grammars not pleasing him, he
prepared one himself for his pupils.   The duties
of his office kept him too busy to write, and only
some translations from the Spanish and a prose
work, *Outre-Mer*, represent this period.   *Outre-Mer*
means " Beyond the Sea," and the book is a collection of sketches he had gathered while traveling.
His prose does not equal his poetry by any means.
Harvard College asked him to become one of her
faculty, and there was a second trip to Europe to
study, this time to Holland and the northern portion.   After seventeen years as professor in Harvard
he resigned; but he continued to live in the town of
Cambridge, in the famous Craigie House.   Washington had once his headquarters there, and when the

new professor first went there to board Washington's room was assigned him.   He afterwards bought the house, and now every visitor to Cambridge goes to see Longfellow's home.   On a third visit to Europe Longfellow met his second wife.   *Hyperion*, a sentimental sketch of travels, tells of this visit.   The hero meets his lady-love just as Longfellow did ; but the story is just a thread running through it.   It is full of legends of the river Rhine, and there are scattered through it several translations of German poems. If one is going to travel on the Rhine it is a pleasant book to have packed in one's shawlstraps.   Though a prose work, the prose is poetical sounding, dreamy, and fanciful.

Poems. — The same year with *Hyperion* (1839), *Voices of the Night* appeared, containing among other pieces *The Reaper and the Flowers* and *The Psalm of Life*, two poems that made their way to every heart.   Mothers from whom " the reaper whose name is Death " had taken fair flowerets "they most did love " were comforted by the new telling of the old thought that they would "find them all again in the fields of light above."   Youths with high hopes and bright ambitions rejoiced in finding their longings put in words in the *Psalm of Life*.   There is nothing strange or startling in the psalm ; it is only the spirit of hope saying to the spirit of despondency :

> " Act, act in the living present,
>   Heart within and God o'erhead ! "

Yet it has been copied, sung, quoted, translated as certainly no other American poem has ever been copied and translated.   We may have heard it until it is stale to us, but the message,

> " Be not like dumb, driven cattle —
>   Be a hero in the strife,"

has roused and still rouses a wish to be greater in young hearts. I have been struck with the fact that elderly people, if not literary, often speak of Longfellow as "the one who wrote the *Psalm of Life.*" A workman on the streets of London stopped Longfellow and asked that he might shake hands with "the man who wrote the *Psalm of Life.*" It is said that in the interior of Asia the poem is found in the speech of those remote nations.

Why is his Poetry so Popular ?—George William Curtis, one of our critics, has given a reason: "His poetry expresses a universal sentiment in the simplest and most melodious manner." The majority of people will always read and love the works of any one who thinks and feels as they think and feel, and who can put those thoughts and feelings in fitting, beautiful words. Critics may say that Longfellow is not grand; that he utters nothing which ordinary folks, anybody and everybody, did not know and believe before he uttered it: but they cannot say that any one else has uttered it more gracefully and pleasingly.

It would be impossible to mention all his short popular pieces, as *The Building of the Ship, The Skeleton in Armor, Santa Filomena*, but he wrote a great many that will probably occur to every memory. His verse easily lends itself to music, and *The Day is Done, The Bridge*, and *The Rainy Day* are well-known songs. As learned as Longfellow was, his style is very simple. He sings clearly, and through each poem throbs one idea. This is why children like his pieces so well. The children of Cambridge felt that he was their special friend, and when the "spreading chestnut tree" under which the smithy stood in *The Village Blacksmith* had to be cut down, they had it made into an armchair and gave it to him on his birthday.   Both Longfellow and Whittier wrote poems about this chair.

Longfellow was not like Whittier in being just a lyric or ballad writer.   There is hardly any style that was not used by him, and in three poems he used two peculiar forms which no one had supposed would suit English.   It is on these three that his fame most depends: *Evangeline, The Courtship of Miles Standish*, and *Hiawatha*.   The first two are written in what is called "hexameter" verse.   There are thirteen to seventeen syllables in a line, making it very long.   It is the meter which the Greek poet Homer and the Latin poet Virgil used.

The meter of "Hiawatha" is quaint, being like that of uncivilized nations in their poetical legends. There is no rhyme, and there are many repetitions in the lines.   It suited the subject, for *Hiawatha* is an Indian epic, and is modeled after an old, old epic, the *Kalevala* of Finland.   Longfellow studied the stories of the Indians, and selecting the best, connected them with his hero Hiawatha, belonging to the Ojibway tribe near Lake Superior.   The poem tells of woods and birds, canoes and wigwams; of Hiawatha's boyhood, his learning the speech of all the animals, his first hunt, his meeting and marrying his beautiful Minnehaha; of a dreadful famine; of Minnehaha's death; of all that befell Hiawatha, who is as grand as any of Cooper's Indians.

The story of "Evangeline" goes back to 1755, when the English took Nova Scotia from the French, —it was called Acadie then,—drove out the poor people settled there, and burned their homes.   Evangeline, a fair, saintly maiden, becomes separated from the young blacksmith to whom she is engaged, and seeks him for years through the forests and prairies of this wild, new continent, ever missing him, though hearing of him, till at last she finds him in a hospital dying. It was at a dinner that the story was suggested to Longfellow by Hawthorne, who had thought of writing a novel with some such plot; he gave up the plan and it was adopted by Longfellow.

"**The Courtship of Miles Standish**" relates a story of two of Longfellow's ancestors, John Alden and Priscilla Mullens, two of the "Mayflower" Puritans. Captain Miles Standish, a better warrior than lover, sent his secretary, John Alden, to Priscilla to address her for him. John Alden went most reluctantly, for he was in love with Priscilla himself, as Priscilla well knew. He found her sitting at her spinning wheel, and faithfully delivered the message, loyally praising the grim captain and urging his claims; but Priscilla looked up slyly and asked, "Why don't you speak for yourself, John?" The result of course made Miles Standish angry. He disappears after a while, but just as Priscilla and Alden are being married comes back, much to their alarm. He is cured, however, of both his love and his anger, and gives his blessing to the young couple.

Longfellow's happy, happy life—"too happy," he says of it—was saddened by an awful event. His wife, while sealing a letter with wax, caught fire from the lighted taper, and burned to death in the presence of her husband and children. That this grief was ever with him afterwards, we know from his pathetic *Via Solitaria* —"The Solitary Way;" but it made him gentler, if that were possible, and sweeter, although sadder. To solace himself he began the translation of the great work of the famous Italian poet Dante,[1] and succeeded as no one

[1] Dante, the greatest Italian poet, and one of the greatest of the world. He lived in the thirteenth century; wrote the *Divina Commedia*, describing "heaven, hell, and purgatory."

else has.   It is told that he did this task as he stood by his desk every morning waiting for his coffee to boil.

Translations.— No other scholar or writer has done so much to give to us the culture of Europe by putting into our tongue choice selections from foreign poets.   His *Poets and Poetry of Europe*, containing a large number of translations and very helpful notes and criticisms, has brought to us many favorite pieces which we might never have heard of otherwise. Very lovely for children is *The Children of the Lord's Supper*, taken from the Swedish, and representing a Swedish confirmation scene at Pentecost, the day when the young "at the foot of the altar renew the vows of their baptism."

"On the right the boys had their places,
　　Delicate figures, with close-curling hair, and cheeks
　　　　rosy blooming;
　　But on the left hand of these there stood the tremu-
　　　　lous lilies,
　　Tinged with the blushing light of the morning, the
　　　　diffident maidens,

　　　·　　　　·　　　　·　　　　·　　　　·　　　　·

　　Knee against knee they knitted a wreath round the
　　　　altar's inclosure."

Saucy and airy is *Beware!* from the German:

　　　　" I know a maiden fair to see,
　　　　　　Take care !

　　　　　·　　　　·　　　　·　　　　·

　　　　She has two eyes so soft and brown,
　　　　　　Take care !
　　　　She gives a side-glance and looks down,
　　　　　　Beware !   Beware !
　　　　　　Trust her not,
　　　　She is fooling thee ! "

Other Poems.—Just as he wrote in almost all styles, he wrote on all subjects. *Tales of a Wayside Inn* is a collection of tales told by travelers at an inn. *Paul Revere's Ride* is one of these tales; the legends of *King Olaf* of Norway are even better told. *The Golden Legend* goes back to the thirteenth century. *The Divine Tragedy* is on the life of Christ. *The Spanish Student* is in a dramatic form, and *Michael Angelo* is a tragedy not published until after the poet's death.

Honors.—Longfellow, in company with his daughters, paid his fourth visit to Europe, everywhere being received with honors. A little incident that occurred at Queen Victoria's royal residence gratified him as much as the Queen's graciously kind reception: the servants stood in the halls and at the door to see him, because, as Victoria explained, they had heard her husband, Prince Albert, read *Evangeline* to the children. England has put his bust in the Poets' Corner of Westminster Abbey—the highest mark of esteem. He is as much read there as here, and to many foreigners he is the *one* American poet. At home Longfellow had one rare tribute of love paid him: his seventy-fifth birthday was celebrated by the schoolchildren. When he passed away soon afterwards, March 24, 1882, school after school reverently draped their halls in mourning, and even now from Maine to Florida, from Massachusetts to California, thousands of schoolchildren keep the 27th of February as Longfellow's day.

Summary.—HENRY WADSWORTH LONGFELLOW (1807–82), born on February 27, at Portland, Maine; died March 24, in Cambridge, Massachusetts, his home for more than forty years. He is our best-known, and has been our most prolific, poet. Was graduated at Bowdoin College, Maine; was professor of modern languages there, and afterwards at Harvard. Was in Europe four times.

Works: Evangeline, Hiawatha, Courtship of Miles Standish, Tales of a Wayside Inn, The Golden Legend, etc.

Short Poems: Psalm of Life, The Reaper and the Flowers, Resignation, The Children's Hour, The Building of the Ship, The Ladder of St. Augustine, The Bridge, The Village Blacksmith, and more than a hundred others.

Prose: Outre-Mer, Hyperion, Kavanagh.

Translations: Dante's *Divina Commedia;* several poems in *Poets and Poetry of Europe,* a collection of translations.

Familiar Quotations from Longfellow.

Lives of great men all remind us,
    We can make our lives sublime;
And, departing, leave behind us
    Footprints on the sands of time;
Footprints, that perhaps another,
    Sailing o'er life's solemn main,
A forlorn and shipwrecked brother,
    Seeing, may take heart again.
                        PSALM OF LIFE.

Thou too, sail on, O Ship of State,
Sail on, O Union, strong and great!
Humanity, with all its fears,
With all its hopes of future years,
Is hanging breathless on thy fate!
            THE BUILDING OF THE SHIP.

There is no flock, however watched and tended,
    But one dead lamb is there!
There is no fireside, howsoe'er defended,
    But has one vacant chair!
                        RESIGNATION.

O not in cruelty, not in wrath,
　　The reaper came that day !
'Twas an angel visited the green earth,
　　And took the flowers away.
　　　　THE REAPER AND THE FLOWERS.

Thus at the flaming forge of life
　　Our fortunes must be wrought:
Thus on its sounding anvil shaped
　　Each burning deed and thought!
　　　　THE VILLAGE BLACKSMITH.

The heights by great men reached and kept
　　Were not attained by sudden flight;
But they, while their companions slept,
　　Were toiling upward in the night.
　　　　THE LADDER OF ST. AUGUSTINE.

'Twas but a dream, — let it pass, — let it vanish like
　　snow;
What I thought was a flower is only a weed, and is
　　worthless !
　　　　COURTSHIP OF MILES STANDISH.

Silently, one by one, in the infinite meadows of heaven,
Blossomed the lovely stars, the forget-me-nots of the
　　Angels.
　　　　　　　　EVANGELINE.

O fear not in a world like this,
　　And thou shalt know, ere long,
Know how sublime a thing it is
　　To suffer and be strong.
　　　　THE LIGHT OF STARS.

All are architects of Fate,
　　Working in these walls of Time ;
Some with massive deeds and great,
　　Some with ornaments of rhyme.
　　　　THE BUILDERS.

CHAPTER XVIII.

How shall he be Classed ?—Though Longfellow and Whittier sometimes used prose, we think of them first and always as poets; but several of the other great authors of the middle fifty years of our century—from about 1825 to 1875 and later—can be classed among either the poetical writers or prose writers. Especially is this true of Oliver Wendell Holmes and James Russell Lowell, who were versatile, or talented in a great many directions, doing equally well in everything they tried. So true is this of Holmes that he has to be put in a class by himself, for he is distinguished as a poet, an essayist, a novelist, a biographer, a wit, a scientist, a professor, and a physician.

His life was such a smoothly successful one that there is little to say in sketching it. He was born at Cambridge, Massachusetts, Aug. 29, 1809, his father being the Rev. Abiel Holmes, for forty years pastor of the Congregational church there, and also a professor at Harvard and an historian. Thus he began "with a first-rate fit-out," with the "four or five generations of gentlemen and gentlewomen," and "the tumbling about in a library as a child," which he mentions somewhere as the advantages a "man of family" possesses. Another sentence of his applies to his childhood: "I like books. I was born and bred among them, and have the easy feeling when I

120

get into their presence that a stable boy has among horses." He had the same enjoyments as other youngsters less fond of books, we judge, however, from this stanza of his:

> "Oh, what are the prizes we perish to win,
>   To the first little 'shiner' we caught with a pin?
> No soil upon earth is so dear to our eyes
> As the soil we first stirred in terrestrial pies!"

He was graduated at Harvard with first honors in 1829, a class we know about from Holmes's own poems, for thirty of his poems were written for reunions of this class. *The Boys*, or "Has any old fellow got mixed with the boys?" is well known. It describes very wittily several of his classmates, some of whom were distinguished men. Among these are the Rev. S. F. Smith, who wrote *My Country, 'tis of Thee*, and Peirce the astronomer. His college friendships lasted through life, and all his first poems were published in the Harvard magazine, the *Collegian*. These were short, witty pieces. Some of them he wrote while studying at law, for he was another in the list of our authors who tried law and gave it up. He did not begin a literary life immediately, but took up medicine, studying it both in Boston and in Europe. He most enthusiastically followed his profession, and was one of the most eminent physicians of Boston, where he lived for more than fifty years. He wrote prize essays on fever and such subjects, and other medical works, making the very heaviest and driest subjects interesting. He learned all about the microscope and the stethoscope, and so skilled was he in anatomy and physiology that he was made professor of these two studies first at Dartmouth, then at Harvard. His students said that he knew how to dissect the human body, and how the blood-vessels run, and how the nerves act, as well as he knew how to dissect the human heart and mind, with its motives and workings.

His First Poems. — But literature has nothing to do with his work as a physician and professor; it is only of his writings you are learning. The first time he wrote for people besides those who took the *Collegian* was in 1830, when it was proposed to break up the frigate "Constitution," a ship that had been in the naval fights of 1812, and had become too old to use. Holmes, by his *Old Ironsides*, beginning, "Ay, tear her tattered ensign down," appealed to the people to save her, and she was saved. The year he took his degree of M.D. at Harvard a volume of his poetry was published, and in it was a comic piece, *My Aunt*, which amused everybody, and *The Last Leaf*, which immediately became a popular song. Of all the men who helped to found American literature, who have made it, shaped it, lifted it up to such a plane that we are not ashamed to compare it with that of other nations, Dr. Holmes lingered the longest among us. *The Last Leaf*, therefore, he often said, suited himself, but it is only some lines of it, as —

> " The names he loved to hear
> Have been carved for many a year
> On the tomb."

Certainly only increasing honor and reverence were felt for him to the very last day of his life. The last stanza did not prove true in its closing lines :

> " And if I should live to be
> The last leaf upon the tree,
> Let them smile as I do now
> At the old forsaken bough
> Where I cling."

"The Autocrat of the Breakfast Table."— In the midst of his busy professional career he sent every now and then a sparkling poem to the *North American Review*. But the work for which he is read, loved, and quoted, and by which he will be known to future generations, began in 1857, at the same time with the *Atlantic Monthly*. He was one of the projectors of the *Atlantic*, choosing its name, and during the rest of his life was so closely associated with it that if we think of one we think of the other. This first year he began a series of essays, which was afterwards put in book form, and this book, *The Autocrat of the Breakfast Table*, has given to Dr. Holmes his pet name, for he is called "The Autocrat" almost as often as by his own name. The Autocrat is a delightful gentleman who relates to us the conversation at the breakfast table of his boarding house, this conversation being almost entirely his own. Indeed he says: "My dear friends, one and all, I can do nothing but report such remarks as I happen to have made at the breakfast table." There are other characters— a sweet young schoolmistress, for instance, who furnishes the material for a tiny thread of a love story, and there is at the close a wedding morning when the Autocrat takes her away as a bride. But all the other boarders are introduced just to supply occasions for flashes of wit, or to give the Autocrat a text for his talk. Thus Dr. Holmes had a new way to express his thoughts, feelings, and observations on life. The book is full of bright sayings and strong, healthful sayings, for the Autocrat hated show and affectation, was most anxious for his countrymen to speak good English and gain true culture, believed in womanhood, and loved truth, honor, and justice. Occasionally the Autocrat repeats a poem composed by himself or some of the characters, and these poems scattered through the book are among the best Dr. Holmes ever wrote. *The Deacon's Masterpiece, or The Wonderful One-hoss Shay,* is his masterpiece in wit. This chaise was built by the deacon so that "it couldn' break daown," for:

> "He made it so like in every part
>   That there wasn't a chance for one to start;
>   For the wheels were just as strong as the thills,
>   And the floor was just as strong as the sills;"

and all the same way through hub, tire and felly, spring, and crossbar. "It ran a hundred years to a day," never breaking down, but gradually wearing out, until finally as the parson was taking a drive and "was working his Sunday's text," "all at once" there was "a shiver and then a thrill," "then something decidedly like a spill;" for the poor old chaise had gone "to pieces—

> "All at once and nothing first,
>   Just as bubbles do when they burst."

"The Chambered Nautilus" shows another side, a higher side, of our Autocrat's talent, and it is said that it was his wish to be remembered by it rather than by anything else. This species of nautilus has a shell full of sections, each section of the spiral—for the shell is shaped in a widening spiral—being larger than the one which precedes it, and as the little creature grows it changes from one of the smaller chambers to a larger. The sight of such a shell suggested the beautiful stanzas. Of the final stanza we can well repeat to the author his own words to the cast-up shell: "Thanks for the heavenly message brought by thee." Is not this message inspiring?

"Build thee more stately mansions, O my soul,
　　As the swift seasons roll!
　　Leave thy low-vaulted past!
Let each new temple, nobler than the last,
Shut thee from heaven with a dome more vast,
　　Till thou at length art free,
Leaving thine outgrown shell by life's unresting sea!"

The Poet and the Professor. — Two of the boarders at the breakfast table of the Autocrat were a poet
and a professor, and readers were so charmed with
this new and breezy style that *The Autocrat* was
followed by *The Professor at the Breakfast Table*,
and fifteen years later by *The Poet at the Breakfast Table*, Dr. Holmes being in one the Poet, and
in the other the Professor. They are not so widely
known, and critics do not agree as to their merits.
There are some very pathetic touches in *The Professor*, for in it there is a little, deformed gentleman
to whom a beautiful young girl only seventeen or
eighteen is drawn because of her warm, sympa-
thetic nature. The deformed gentleman becomes
ill, and the girl helps the Professor to care for
him. The dying man said, one day, in describing
the utter sadness of his life: "'Since my mother
kissed me before she died no woman's lips have
pressed my cheek, nor ever will.' The young girl's
eyes glitter with a sudden film, and almost without a
thought, but with a warm human instinct that rushed
up into her face with her heart's blood, she bent over
and kissed him. It was a sacrament that washed
out long years of bitterness, and I should hold it an
unworthy thought to defend her. The little gentleman repaid her with the only tear any of us ever saw
him shed."

His Novels and Later Works. — You see he can
be tender as well as humorous; but he is at his best

in this style of half essay, not in novels, for there is something unnatural about his *Elsie Venner.* In both it and *The Guardian Angel* Dr. Holmes takes up psychological subjects, and some of his shrewdest sentences sound of his profession. His memoirs of Motley and of Emerson are enjoyable. He sent forth other collections of papers from the *Atlantic Monthly*, as *Soundings from the Atlantic* and *Over the Teacups.* He also wrote some volumes of poetry, as *Songs in Many Keys* and *The Iron Gate*, and several scientific works, one being on the brain. So often was he called on for verses for special occasions that the title "The Poet Laureate of America" fits him. There are perhaps a hundred poems for commencements, class reunions, etc., that he has written. He was selected to write the *Welcome to the Nations* at the Centennial of 1876; and the dedicatory poem for the fountain erected by an American at Stratford-on-Avon is by him.

When he visited Europe not so very many years ago he was welcomed with many honors, Oxford conferring a degree on him. On his seventieth birthday the *Atlantic Monthly* publishers, to show their appreciation of what he had done for that magazine, gave him a breakfast at which were gathered the writers of our country, and then were showered upon him tributes from other poets and other prose writers. When he died on the 7th of October, 1894, a universal sadness filled our hearts. He was the last of the famous group that founded our literature.

Summary.—OLIVER WENDELL HOLMES (1809–94). Born in Cambridge; long a resident of Boston; physician, poet, wit, essayist; wrote for the *Atlantic Monthly* from its beginning in 1857.

Prose Works : Essays : *Autocrat of the Breakfast Table, Professor at the Breakfast Table, Poet at the Breakfast Table, Soundings from the Atlantic, Over the Teacups.* Novels : *Elsie Venner* and *Guardian Angel.* Memoirs : Emerson and Motley. Scientific and medical papers.

Poems : *Songs in Many Keys, Songs of Many Seasons, Urania,* and *The Iron Gate.* Wrote many pieces for special occasions. Well-known single poems : *The Wonderful One-hoss Shay, The Chambered Nautilus, The Last Leaf, My Aunt, Bill and Joe, Old Ironsides,* and many others.

Some Sparkles from Holmes.

I find the great thing in this world is not so much where we stand as in what direction we are moving.

I would have a woman as true as death. At the first lie which works from the heart outward she should be tenderly chloroformed into a better world, where she can have an angel for a governess, and feed on strange fruits, which shall make her all over again, even to her bones and marrow.

Sin has many tools, but a lie is a handle which fits them all.

No stranger can get a great many notes of torture out of a human soul ; it takes one that knows it well — parent, child, brother, sister, intimate.

"Self-made" is imperfectly made, or education is a superfluity and a failure.

Talking is one of the fine arts, — the noblest, the most important, the most difficult, — and its fluent harmonics may be spoiled by the intrusion of a single harsh note.

Society is a strong solution of books. It draws the virtue out of what is best worth reading, as hot water draws the strength of tea leaves.

A man's opinions are generally of much more value than his arguments.

Controversy equalizes fools and wise men in the same way — and the fools know it.

You may set it down as a truth which admits of few exceptions that those who ask your opinion really want your praise.

Fame usually comes to those who are thinking about something else; rarely to those who say to themselves, "Go to, now! let us be a celebrated individual!"

Memory is a net. One finds it full of fish when he takes it from the brook, but a dozen miles of water have run through it without sticking.

> Soft is the breath of a maiden's Yes:
> Not the light gossamer stirs with less;
> But never a cable holds so fast
> Through all the battles of wave and blast.

Why should we look one common faith to find
When one in every score is color-blind?
If here on earth they know not red from green,
Will they see better into things unseen?

> Oh, could there in this world be found
> Some little spot of happy ground,
> Without the village tattling.

> Oh, that the mischief-making crew
> Were all reduced to one or two,
> And they were painted red or blue,
> That every one might know them!

Thou, O my country, hast thy foolish ways!
Too apt to purr at every stranger's praise;
But if the stranger touch thy modes or laws,
Off goes the velvet, and out come the claws.

Youth longs and Manhood strives; but Age remembers:
  Sits by the raked-up ashes of the past,
Spreads its thin hands above the whitening embers
  That warm its creeping life-blood till the last.

CHAPTER XIX.

JAMES RUSSELL LOWELL, POET, CRITIC, ESSAYIST.

Our best critic, and one of our best poets, essayists, and lecturers, was James Russell Lowell. He excelled in every department of literature he attempted; he is counted among our half-dozen real humorists; and he ranked high in public affairs as one of our foreign ministers. He, too, was the son of a clergyman of Cambridge, and he, too, belonged to a gentle, refined, literary family. He was ten years younger than Holmes, being born in 1819, on Washington's birthday, February 22. Education was one of the chief rights demanded by and for the young members of the Lowell family, and there was no advantage denied this boy. But he was not at first ready to make use of these advantages as his teachers thought he ought. It is hard to realize that such a worker in after years was ever regarded as "indolent" and "a dreamer;" but he selected his own reading, did not study at Harvard, and for some prank was "rusticated" for a while. He returned and was graduated, being class poet.

When he left college he went to work, first trying law, which, like Bryant and other poets, he disliked, but soon finding his true vocation, the literary one. His first volume of poetry, *A Year's Life*, was published in 1841. Two years later he, Poe, Hawthorne, and Whittier tried to edit a magazine together. Only three numbers of this magazine were issued. Lowell then threw himself into the antislavery cause. The secret of his warm interest in abolitionism was his marriage to an ardent abolitionist, Maria White, herself somewhat of a poet. This marriage when he was only twenty-five made him work harder, and sometimes it was difficult to live within his little literary income. His father's home was the "historical Elmwood," and on the same piece of property a cottage for the young couple was erected, the cottage being named "Elmwood, Junior." It is interesting to read one of his letters of that time: "All I ask is enough for necessaries: . . . my new book will pay me one hundred dollars for the first edition if it sells well; my volume of poetry may be called fifty dollars a year more. . . . The antislavery Friends pay me five dollars for a leader to their paper, which comes out once a fortnight. . . . You see I am not in want." But another letter is not so cheerful: "I am often down in the mouth; but sometimes at the end of a year, when I have done a tolerable share of work and have nothing to show for it, I feel as if I had rather be a clerk than a man of letters."

Success was on the way to him. In 1848 he gave to the world three of his best-known and most remarkable poems — *The Vision of Sir Launfal, The Biglow Papers,* and *A Fable for Critics,* — remarkable because so totally different in style and thought. The first was of a deeply moral and religious character; the second and third were very witty, one full of purposed bad spelling, bad grammar, and slang, with the bitterest sarcasms against slavery, the other kindly and humorously satirical, and about living authors of his day.

"The Vision of Sir Launfal" relates to the old and favorite legend of the Holy Grail,[1] but our poet has

---

[1] The Holy Grail, or San Graal, was, according to the legend, the cup used by our Saviour when He instituted the Lord's

treated it as no other writer has done. Sir Launfal, in the flush of youth, health, and wealth, sets out on his quest for the cup, and as he rides forth scornfully flings alms to a beggar at his gate. Long afterwards he returns, poor and homeless, almost a beggar himself, the search for the cup having proved a failure. A poor leper is by the roadside. No longer scornful, the disappointed pilgrim divides his molded crust with the leper, and going to the brook brings him water in a wooden bowl. As he lifts his bowl to the leper's lips it suddenly turns to the Grail itself, the leper who stands before him is the Saviour, and he learns the lesson:

> "Who gives himself with his alms feeds three —
> Himself, his hungry neighbor, and Me."

But it is neither the story nor the religious sentiment that makes *The Vision of Sir Launfal* so beautiful; it is the opening description of June. So fine is this that you can hear the birds singing and see the "clods climb to life in grass and flowers;" you can "hear life murmur and see it glisten." If you live in the South you should read it in May or in April, when spring is at its best, and you can

> "Sit in the warm shade and feel right well,
> How the sap creeps up and the blossoms swell."

In **"A Fable for Critics"** Bryant, Hawthorne, and Whittier are hit off very well; and Emerson, Longfellow, Irving, Poe, and Margaret Fuller are

Supper, and was kept by Joseph of Arimathea. At last it was hidden away, and no one except a perfectly pure, upright character could find it.

described in a sharp, funny way. As there was no name to the satire, he gave his own portrait:

"Here's Lowell, who's striving Parnassus to climb,
    With a whole bale of isms tied together with rhyme:
    The top of the hill he'll ne'er come nigh reaching
    Till he learns the distinction between singing and
        preaching."

The chief "ism" in this bale was patriotism, for all his life he tried to rouse his fellow-citizens to love their country's honor and welfare more than party or their own selfish interests. Every poem except the *Fable for Critics* was a "preaching" of some clear, high truth, and the truth was to him more important than the poem itself.

The one ism in the " Biglow Papers " is abolitionism. He had made passionate appeals against slavery, he had delivered strong protests against it, but they were not heeded as he wished; he therefore looked into his mind to find some literary weapon sharp enough. He determined to use wit, and he succeeded. *The Biglow Papers* set people to laughing, but from reading and laughing they ended in agreeing with the sentiments and ideas. Lowell was next to Whittier in the help which he gave by poems to the cause. There are two series of *The Biglow Papers*, one against the Mexican War and the other written during the Civil War, but both are about slavery. The name is from Hosea Biglow, one of the characters, who is represented as giving his views in his own peculiar dialect, that of an uneducated Yankee farmer. Other people, as Birdofredum Sawin and the good preacher Homer Wilbur, express their ideas or insert remarks. Much of the poem is out of date now, and the local hits at people then living cannot now be enjoyed or understood. But some of the lines are

as fresh and true to-day as they were then. We still
have among us the self-important politician who

"Sez the world'll go right ef he hollers out 'Gee!'"

and the slippery politician who thinks

"A ginooine statesman must be on his guard
Ef he must hev beliefs not to b'leeve them tu hard;"

but even more common is that low class of political
office-seekers and bosses who "*don't* believe in prin-
cerple, but, oh, they *du* in interest." How true it is
still of such a man that he

"Has ben on all sides that give places or pelf;

　・　　　・　　　・　　　・　　　・　　　・

He's ben true to *one* party, an' thet is himself."

Not only are politicians well advised in this poem —
there is a fine motto in it which every boy or girl
should remember in working and studying:

"Folks thet worked thorough was the ones thet thriv,
But bad work follers ye ez long's ye live;
But can't git red on 't — jest ez sure ez sin
It's ollers askin' to be done agin."

There is a striking thought in a dialogue between the
United States and England, personated by Uncle
Sam and John Bull:

"Old Uncle S., sez he, 'I guess
God's price is high,' sez he.
'But nothin' else than wut he sells
Wears long.'"

"The Atlantic Monthly."— But I did not intend
to forget Lowell himself in telling about these three
pieces. He was offered Longfellow's place at Har-

vard, and to prepare for it went to Dresden, Germany. But when he came back something he liked better than teaching engaged his attention. He, with Longfellow, Emerson, and Holmes, founded the *Atlantic Monthly*, and Lowell was chosen its editor. The names of the men who founded it indicate the high standard which such a literary magazine would have. In its pages some of our finest literature has first appeared. For ten years Lowell was joint editor of the *North American Review*, and the essays written for these and other periodicals make up the greater portion of his prose works. There are four volumes of essays : *Among my Books* (two volumes), *My Study Windows*, and *Fireside Travels*.

Essays. — There is a mixture of subjects in *My Study Windows*. The author talks of various English poets, speaks *A Good Word for Winter*, and chats of *My Garden Acquaintance*. You would enjoy an introduction to his garden acquaintances, " the birds and the squirrels." He said once, but it was in his early life, that he valued his "poetry at a thousand times " his prose ; but America owes most of all to his scholarly criticisms. He had read so deeply and so well that by his lectures and essays he became a literary educator ; that is, he taught both by precept and practice what is good writing, and he helped readers to make a wise choice of good reading. His rare gift of speech and still rarer fund of knowledge are apparent in his criticisms, though the knowledge is so deep that it sometimes keeps people who are *not* well read from understanding them altogether. On his return from Europe he delivered twelve lectures on the British poets.

He was sent to Spain as minister by our government, and afterwards transferred to England, where he charmed the English people by his knightly polite-

ness and brilliant talents.   He delivered a good many
orations and addresses in England, and these are
now collected in a volume entitled *Democracy and
other Addresses.*   England has honored him greatly.
In Westminster Abbey there is a tablet to his memory,
and both Oxford and Cambridge conferred degrees
on him.   He loved England, going back several
times after he ceased to be minister there; but his
own country was first in his affections, and most
earnestly did he try to lift her politically as well as
intellectually, for he had strong, outspoken opinions
in politics as in literature.   America lost a true patriot
when he died, in 1891.

Other volumes of his poems include *The Cathedral,
Under the Willows,* and *Heartsease and Rue.*   Everybody has heard one of his short pieces, *The First
Snowfall,* which tells of the first snow that fell on his
little one's grave, and of little Mabel's question, " Father, who makes it snow ? "   *The Changeling* is about
this same little one that died, and so is a sweet piece
of poetry, *The Morning Glory,* written by his wife.
The grandest of Lowell's efforts are two " Odes" —
the *Harvard Commemoration Ode,* in honor of the
Harvard men who died in the war, and one to celebrate the hundredth anniversary of the Concord fight.
Since his death a volume of his letters has been published, and they are delightfully written.

Summary. — JAMES RUSSELL LOWELL (1819–91),
  poet, essayist, humorist, lecturer, a " scholar in
  politics," and our finest critic.   Birthplace and
  home, Cambridge, Massachusetts.   Educated at
  Harvard; entered literary life; ardent abolitionist; went to Germany to study; first editor of
  Atlantic Monthly; joint editor of *North American
  Review;* minister to Spain and to England.

Prose Works: Essays: *My Study Windows, Among my Books, Fireside Travels, Democracy and other Addresses.*

Poems: Biglow Papers, humorous and political; *A Fable for Critics, The Vision of Sir Launfal, The Cathedral, Under the Willows, Heartsease and Rue, Harvard Commemoration Ode* and *Concord Centennial Ode, The Present Crisis, The Changeling,* and *The First Snowfall.*

Common Quotations from Lowell.

Since, with thy love, this knowledge too was given,
Which each calm day doth strengthen more and more,
That they who love are but one step from heaven.

Great truths are portions of the soul of man;
Great souls are portions of Eternity.

Be noble! and the nobleness that lies
In other men, sleeping, but never dead,
Will rise in majesty to meet thine own.
                                        SONNETS.

True love is but a humble, low-born thing,
And hath its food served up in earthenware;
It is a thing to walk with, hand in hand,
Through the everydayness of this workday world;
    .   .   .   .   .   .
A simple fireside thing, whose quiet smile
Can warm earth's poorest hovel to a home.
                                        LOVE.

Yet in herself she dwelleth not,
    Although no home were half so fair;
No simplest duty is forgot;
Life hath no dim and lowly spot
    That doth not in her sunshine share.

She doeth little kindnesses
   Which most leave undone or despise;
For naught that sets our heart at ease,
And giveth happiness or peace,
   Is low esteemèd in her eyes.

    .   .   .   .   .

Blessing she is.   God made her so,
And deeds of week-day holiness
Fall from her noiseless as the snow.
                         NOT AS OTHERS.

   Daily with souls that cringe and plot
   We Sinais climb, and know it not.

Earth gets its price for what earth gives us:
    .   .   .   .   .

At the devil's booth are all things sold:
Each ounce of dross costs its ounce of gold;
For a cap and bells our lives we pay;
   Bubbles we buy with a whole soul's tasking;
'Tis heaven alone that is given away,
   'Tis only God can be had for the asking.
No price is set on the lavish summer;
June may be had by the poorest comer.
And what is so rare as a day in June?
   Then, if ever, come perfect days;
Then Heaven tries the earth if it be in tune,
   And over it softly her warm ear lays.

    .   .   .   .   .

The little bird sits at his door in the sun,
Atilt like a blossom among the leaves;
    .   .   .   .   .

His mate feels the eggs beneath her wings,
And the heart in her dumb breast flutters and sings:
He sings to the wide world, she to her nest,—
In the nice ear of Nature which song is the best?
               VISION OF SIR LAUNFAL.

   They are slaves who dare not be
   In the right with two or three.

Truth forever on the scaffold, Wrong forever on the throne;
Yet that scaffold sways the future, and behind the dim
    unknown
Standeth God within the shadow, keeping watch above his
    own.

                    THE PRESENT CRISIS.

Folks thet's afeard to fail are sure of failin':
God hates your sneakin' creturs thet believe
He'll settle things they run away and leave.

    To say why gals act so or so,
      Or don't, 'ould be presumin';
    Mebby to mean *yes* an' say *no*
    Comes nateral to woman.

                  THE BIGLOW PAPERS.

Nothing takes longer in saying than anything else.
All the beautiful sentiments in the world weigh less than
a single lovely action.
Be a man among men, not a humbug among humbugs.
Large charity doth never soil, but only whiten, soft
white hands.
Not failure, but low aim, is crime.

*Extract from one of Lowell's letters, in which he de-
scribes a speech of Emerson's.*

Emerson's oration was more disjointed than usual even
with him. It began nowhere and ended everywhere; and
yet, as always with that divine man, it left you feeling that
something beautiful had passed that way — something
more beautiful than anything else, like the rising and setting
of stars. Every possible criticism might have been made
on it but one — that it was not noble. There was a tone
in it that awakened all elevating associations. He bog-
gled, he lost his place, he had to put on his glasses; but
it was as if a creature from some fairer world had lost his
way in our fogs, and it was our fault, not his. It was
chaotic, but it was all such stuff as stars are made of. . . .
All through it I felt something in me that cried, " Ha, ha,
to the sound of the trumpets ! "

CHAPTER XX.

A Self-made Man.—There died, in 1878, at Berlin, a writer who, though yet in the prime of his life, was the author of thirty-seven books, all good. He was, moreover, the master of a score of languages, a traveler who had visited every habitable part of the globe, a lecturer whom all delighted to hear. He could look back on all these acquirements as his own, for he was a self-educated, self-made man, and yet, strange to say, a disappointed man. Bayard Taylor, for such was his name, had one ambition, to be a *great* poet. He looked upon all other accomplishments only as stepping stones to that, and he did not even like to hear of his prose works. These he called contemptuously "potboilers;" they were only to support him. Into his poems went his soul—all, as he himself said, that he was or hoped to be. Some of them show almost genius. In all our literature no more remarkable example of pluck, perseverance, and giant work can be found. His native place, Kennett Square, Chester County, Pennsylvania, was a little country village where the poor boy could obtain only a few years of common-school education. At seventeen he went out into the world for himself. Just a moneyless apprentice, he had neither friends nor influence, yet he faced his difficulties and over-

139

came them. Even then the longing to be a poet was in his heart, and believing that to be a poet he must see and know, he determined to do both. In spare minutes he studied French and Latin, and wrote occasional verses. To see he must travel, and to travel he must have means — and traveling was more expensive then than now. A position as contributor to a paper would furnish the means. To secure such a position he must have reputation, and to secure the reputation he collected his random verses into a volume entitled *Ximena.* Finally he succeeded in obtaining a conditional order from Horace Greeley [1] for letters to the *Tribune;* and the *Saturday Evening Post* and the *United States Gazette* each paid him fifty dollars in advance for twelve letters to be written from abroad. With the letter from Greeley, the hundred dollars and another forty, he set forth, and remained two years in Europe on the five hundred dollars which his letters of travel brought him.

Books of Travel. —*Views Afoot ; or, Europe seen with Knapsack and Staff,* is the book name of these letters, a book so popular that it went through six editions in one year. It is charmingly written, and has the rare good quality of telling what is important and omitting what is unimportant. On his return Taylor edited a country newspaper a short time, but soon became assistant editor of the *Tribune.* In 1849, the year gold was discovered in California, this paper sent him out to California and Mexico as a traveling correspondent. *El Dorado* was the resulting work. Another trip in the opposite direction took him to lands then almost unknown, for he not only penetrated into the regions beyond the Himalayas, but went far up the Nile into Central Africa, going fifty

[1] Horace Greeley, a prominent man in politics, and the founder and first editor of the New York *Tribune.*

thousand miles in a little more than two years.   Three
books describe this long trip.

He was now very popular as a lecturer, but
he hated the platform, disliking to be stared at as
"the great American traveler."   After two or three
years he made one more trip, going this time north-
ward through Norway and Lapland, where he had a
sight of the sun at midnight.   In 1857 he married
Marie Hansen, the daughter of the distinguished
German astronomer, and settled down near Kennett
Square, at his country home, " Cedarcroft."   He
was then in his thirties, and felt that he might gain
the desire of his heart.   In the daytime he wrote prose
for money and " at night poems for fame."

He finished a round dozen books of travel,
and wrote four novels — *Hannah Thurston, John Godfrey's Fortunes, Joseph and his Friend,* and *The Story
of Kennett.*   The last is an account of his native village.   Some of his volumes of poetry are *Lars : a Pastoral of Norway, The Masque of the Gods,* and *Prince
Deukalion.*   His grandest work is his translation of
Faust[1] from the German, the finest translation of it in
existence, the more beautiful because he has retained
the meters as in the original.   It was a labor of several
years, and we wonder sadly as we read it whether his
own rank as a poet would not have been higher if he
had had more leisure.   Sent by the government on an
embassy to Germany, he died there in 1878.

Some of Taylor's pieces are very popular.   The
Song of the Camp is a simple little incident happening in camp on the night before the storming of the
forts at Sebastopol.   " Give us a song ! " the soldiers
cried ;

[1] *Faust,* a drama by the great German poet Goethe.   It is
founded on an old legend in which Faust sells his soul to the
devil in exchange for the power to gain any wish.

> "They sang of love and not of fame;
>   Forgot was Britain's glory;
> Each heart recalled a different name,
>   But all sang 'Annie Laurie.'"

Two couplets from it are especially quoted:

> "Something upon the soldier's cheek
>   Washed off the stains of powder;"

and

> "The bravest are the tenderest,
>   The loving are the daring."

Grand with passion is the *Bedouin Love Song:*

> "I love thee, I love but thee,
>   With a love that shall not die
> Till the sun grows cold,
> And the stars are old,
> And the leaves of the judgment book unfold!"

Amram's Wooing, another poem, is a love story of the desert. *The Quaker Widow* is a favorite. One of his odes was read at the Centennial of the Declaration of Independence.

Josiah Gilbert Holland was no less ambitious and industrious than Taylor, but, not being naturally so talented, his years of drudgery lasted longer. The son of a Massachusetts farmer, he strove for an education, trying first one way to earn money, then another. He taught, tried to be a physician, but, not getting a practice, finally connected himself with the Springfield *Republican,* publishing in its columns several of his works. Especially popular were his letters to young people, signed Timothy Titcomb, and called *The Titcomb Letters.* They must have had an influence on many young men eager for success.

All his novels are on the same line — lessons to young people who are going through an experience like his own. They are not brilliant or strikingly original, but they are healthful and were well liked. His sweetest poems are *Bitter Sweet* and *Katrina*. His permanent lifework is the founding of the *Century Magazine*, of which he was the first editor, though it was then named *Scribner's Monthly*. In it appeared his novels *Arthur Bonnicastle* and *Sevenoaks*.

Holland has expressed for us questions that come to us every time we look at a baby:

> "What is the little one thinking about?
>   Very wonderful things, no doubt;
>   Unwritten history!
>   Unfathomed mystery!
>   Yet he chuckles, and crows, and nods, and winks,
>   As if his head were full of kinks."

Summary. — BAYARD TAYLOR (1825–78). Born in Pennsylvania; traveler, lecturer, poet, novelist. A self-educated man; traveled over habitable globe.

Works: Travels: *Views Afoot, El Dorado, Byways of Europe*, and many others. Miscellaneous: *Studies in German Literature*. Novels: *Hannah Thurston, Story of Kennett*. Poems: *Lars: a Pastoral of Norway, Masque of the Gods, Prince Deukalion*. Shorter pieces: *Song of the Camp, Bedouin Love Song, Amram's Wooing, National Ode*. Translation: *Faust*.

JOSIAH GILBERT HOLLAND (1819–81), poet, novelist, moralist, editor. After a struggling life became editor of *Scribner's Monthly*, now the *Century Magazine*. Prose: *The Titcomb Letters, Arthur Bonnicastle*. Poems: *Katrina, Bitter Sweet*.

A few Lines from Taylor.

Fame is what you have taken,
Character's what you give;
. When to this truth you waken
Then you begin to live.

IMPROVISATIONS.

The hearts that dare are quick to feel;
The hands that wound are soft to heal.

SOLDIERS OF PEACE.

The violet loves the sunny bank,
The cowslip loves the lea;
The scarlet-creeper loves the elm,
But I love — thee.

THE PROPOSAL.

Learn to live and live to learn,
Ignorance like a fire doth burn,
Little tasks make large returns.

TO MY DAUGHTER.

Somewhere above us, in elusive ether,
Lives the fulfillment of our dearest dreams.

A few Lines from Holland.

Heaven is not reached at a single bound,
But we build the ladder by which we rise
From the lowly earth to the vaulted skies,
And we mount to its summit round by round.

I count this thing to be grandly true
That a noble deed is a step toward God,
Lifting the soul from the common clod
To a purer air and a broader view.

We rise by the things that are under our feet;
By what we have mastered of good and gain;
By the pride deposed and the passion slain,
And the vanquished ills that we hourly meet.

GRADATIM.

CHAPTER XXI.

During the War. — Naturally there was not much lasting literature produced during the war; but some stirring or tender songs of that period are still living and ringing, and keeping their authors' names from being entirely forgotten. Such verses as *The Blue and the Gray*, by Francis M. Finch, and *All Quiet along the Potomac*, by Ethel Beers; and such songs as *Maryland, my Maryland*, by James Randall, and *Dixie*, by Albert Pike, still have power to stir our feelings and rouse enthusiasm for the associations which they awaken, if for nothing else. The chorus of *John Brown's Body Lies a-Moldering*, by which the Union soldiers marched, and *The Battle Hymn of the Republic*, by Julia Ward Howe, are in the same meter. *Sheridan's Ride* is by T. Buchanan Read, known as the writer of other poems and as a painter.

The Confederacy had its poet laureate in Father Ryan, a Catholic priest of Georgia. His *Conquered Banner* and *Sword of Lee* are cherished for their sentiments by his fellow Southerners. There is a sadness in all his lines. *Their Story Runneth Thus* is his only long poem.

Another Confederate poet of the same church, Theodore O'Hara of Kentucky, is known for a poem, *The Bivouac of the Dead*, written in honor of the Kentucky soldiers who died in the Mexican War.

So many Northern poets wrote patriotic pieces that no especial one can be singled out. Whittier and

Lowell have already been told about. It has been mentioned also how memoirs, war papers, histories, etc., have flooded the country since 1865. One novel deserves particular notice because of the influence which it had both before and during the war.

" **Uncle Tom's Cabin.**" — No one book of America was ever farther reaching than this novel, *Uncle Tom's Cabin* — farther reaching either literally or figuratively. It has gone into every civilized nation, and it exerted a most powerful political influence in helping to inflame the people of the North against slavery. The writer, Mrs. Harriet Beecher Stowe, belonged to a literary family. Her father was a strong, influential man and preacher, and one of her brothers was the Rev. Henry Ward Beecher, a lecturer, author, and famous preacher. When a child she read a great deal and felt an ambition to write. She read and re-read Walter Scott's novels, in order that she might have a clear, animated style. Heart and soul being enlisted against slavery, she undertook to write a story for the cause of abolitionism. The result was *Uncle Tom's Cabin*, published in the *National Era* of Washington in 1851–52, when she was a woman of forty. It sold by thousands of copies when put in book form, has been translated, it is claimed, into forty languages, has been arranged for the stage, and has given its author enduring fame. Yet it is by no means the story itself nor its style that made it so famous. Her other works, as *The Minister's Wooing* and *Little Foxes*, are better written, perhaps, yet not nearly so widely read. The subject and the time made it create a sensation. Uncle Tom, the hero, is a slave, and the heart-rending incidents introduced show what slavery *could* be in its worst forms. To many it has given their only idea of slavery, and they believe it as if it were true history.

Novels written for a Purpose. — People read stories so much that writers wishing to teach any kind of truth or idea, try to hide it in a story — it is the sugar coating or the capsule which is intended to make the truth more pleasant for the readers to take. High, difficult questions are often thus discussed. Historical facts are taught, views on every subject enforced — fiction serves for all subjects, almost, and for all purposes. The day of the old love story, with its beautiful heroine and interesting hero, its adventures, its hidden plots, and its happy ending, is gone. The novelist, since the war, if not teaching a lesson, is "showing a certain phase of life," "a certain section of country," "some peculiarity in character." Before the war, except that the scenes were laid in America, there was little to distinguish American works of fiction from English. Since the war an American flavor has been added. Distinctively new styles have been cultivated, styles so different that they may be classified. One class treats of commonplace people in commonplace situations — not in a commonplace manner. There is no aim to tell an interesting story, the only object being to analyze the characters of the persons introduced. Another class pictures some little section of the country, the dialect, the customs. Almost every part of our country has thus been described.

This is a prose age rather than a poetical one, no one having arisen to take the place of Whittier or of Longfellow. Those who do sing verses for us sing them in the leisure moments left after a busy day spent in the production of more practical prose. Still more noticeable is it that this is the magazine era — and of our magazines we have a right to be proud, for they excel those of any other country. They discover the most able new writers, and in their pages appear the works of the best living authors. Many of our books — most of them — first appear in the columns of some periodical, and much of our literary culture and taste is due to the high quality of the matter published in the magazines. The founding of the *North American Review* and that of the *Atlantic Monthly* have already been mentioned. In 1850 *Harper's New Monthly Magazine* began; in 1870 the forerunner of the *Century Magazine*, known at first as *Scribner's Monthly*, made its appearance. Now there is a new *Scribner's Magazine.* It is in the magazines that the short story has been developed, until American short stories have, some of them, reached a high degree of excellence. And yet, as the critics say, there is not to-day any great living writer in America whose books will be read in the ages to come. There are dozens whose manner of telling their messages is graceful enough, but the messages are not important enough to be remembered more than a few years. A wise critic, with a practical mind, says: "The test of success is whether the book sells well, is read, talked about, and brings success to the author. We do not demand that which will *wear* well."

Summary. — LITERATURE OF THE WAR: patriotic songs and poems, as *Maryland, my Maryland*, and *Sheridan's Ride. Conquered Banner*, by Father Ryan. *Uncle Tom's Cabin*, a novel against slavery, written by Mrs. Harriet Beecher Stowe (1812).

SINCE THE WAR: *Prose era:* no great poets. *Magazine era:* best authors appear in the leading magazines. Novel has changed from a love story with exciting plot to new styles, the "realistic," "analytic," etc.

CHAPTER XXII.

TWO POETS FROM THE FAR WEST, WALT WHITMAN, AND OTHERS.

Until within the last twenty-five years no voice had been heard from the far West. Until the middle of the century that part of the country was not even settled by Americans. When those regions did begin to be filled by settlers from the older States, it was as in Colonial times — fighting Indians and wild animals, founding towns and building homes, left little time or thought for reading books or writing them. In 1870 two new poets, telling of new scenes, appeared and were hailed with delight by the reading world. One was Bret Harte, poet and story teller of the Rocky Mountains; the other "Joaquin" Miller, poet of the Sierras.

Francis Bret Harte is a native of Albany, New York, the son of a teacher of unusual learning. Early left fatherless, the boy was led by a spirit of adventure to the Rocky Mountain region. It was before order and civilization had reached that country. Cutthroats and gamblers abounded, and lynch law was the rule, not the exception. The youth just from a quiet, bookish home was wonderfully impressed by the strangeness of everything. While he was trying his hand at various ways of earning a living—at school teaching, gold digging, printing, and editing —he was observing and laying up material for his future literary career. At first, however, his attempts in that direction were not the result of his observations, for his *Condensed Novels* consists only of clever, funny parodies on several popular works of fiction.

Stories of the Mines. — It was not until he began editing the *Overland Monthly* of San Francisco that he struck a new, rich vein. In the second number of the magazine was his story, *The Luck of Roaring Camp*, a masterpiece of wit and pathos, and our first picture of a mining camp of the Rockies. The "Luck" was a baby, who, when its wretched, wicked mother died, was left to the care of the rough miners of Roaring Camp. The whole camp felt responsible for the tiny creature, loved it, nursed it, guarded it, and its innocent presence kept back the curses on wicked lips and purified the moral atmosphere of the camp. One night a fearful flood swept down the valley of Roaring Camp; the cabin where the baby was kept was washed away; "the pride, the hope, the joy, the Luck of Roaring Camp had disappeared." The infant was found "cold and pulseless," held in the arms of a miner "cruelly crushed and bruised" — a man who had been the terror of the place, but who had risked his life in the fury of the storm to save the little one. Somebody said of the child, "He is dead." The miner opened his eyes. "Dead?" he repeated, feebly. "Yes, my man, and you are dying too." A smile lit the eyes of the expiring Kentuck. "Dying!" he repeated; "he's a-taking me with him. Tell the boys I've got the Luck with me now." In this as in all of Bret Harte's stories the chief interest is the discovery of the good hidden in the most wicked heart. It is always such a pleasant surprise to find a rough bully showing tenderness as "Kentuck" did in this story. After several months — for he worked in a slow, painstaking fashion — *The Outcasts of Poker Flat* was ready. It is as full as the other of "audacious slang," bad language, fun, pathos, and wild Western life ; and of goodness cropping out, where least expected, in bad men and women. Both stories raised a storm of applause, because they were new and fresh. The mining region and mining ways in 1849 are pictured by him just as they were, though he may have seen a better side than was seen by other lookers-on during the first years of the rush for gold. *The Twins of Table Mountain, How Santa Claus Came to Simpson's Bar, M'liss,* and *Tales of the Argonauts,* are other sketches, all on the same order, bringing both laughter and tears.

An absurd poem lifted Mr. Harte into immediate fame—a piece that he had written as a whim and put in the paper merely to fill up a column. This was called *Plain Language from Truthful James,* but it is better known as *The Heathen Chinee.* It tells of a "Chinee" with "a smile that was childlike and bland," but who was far more cunning than the two white men trying to cheat him at a game of cards, for—

> " In his sleeves, which were long,
>   He had twenty-four packs.
>
> .   .   .   .
>
>   Which is why I remark,
>   And my language is plain,
>   That for ways that are dark
>   And for tricks that are vain,
>   The Heathen Chinee is peculiar ;
>   Which the same I am free to maintain."

The nation laughed, demanded "more," and in 1870 Harte was invited East, and was offered by the *Atlantic Monthly* a very large sum to write exclusively for its pages. His works were now read in Europe as well as in America. He was sent as consul to

Glasgow, Scotland, and has remained abroad almost ever since, a favorite in society, and a prolific writer. But he has never equaled his first half-dozen short stories or his first poems — his freshness is gone. His novels, compared with his short sketches, are failures. He struck a "pocket," not a deep mine, but there was very precious metal in the pocket. *The Society upon the Stanislaus* is richly comical. It and *Dow's Flat* are as purely Western as *The Heathen Chinee*. Quotations can give but little idea of his style.

The poet of the Sierras, "Joaquin" Miller, is really Cincinnatus Heine Miller. His boyhood and youth were exciting enough to furnish material for the most thrilling of romances. His father was a sad, dreamy, big-hearted man, who was always failing in his enterprises, and was always being cheated by less honest men. Utterly discouraged and hopeless, he moved with his family from Indiana to Oregon, a region then inhabited by wild beasts and wild savages. The boy's education was obtained from the reading of a few books, the poet Byron being his special favorite. When a little older he tried mining in California; then he was one of a band of adventurers to Nicaragua; then he joined the Indians, living with them as one of themselves. On going back to civilized people, he was by turns a lawyer, an express messenger, and an editor. His sympathy with the South caused the suppression of his newspaper; and a four years' term as judge ended up the round of occupations which claimed his attention before entering upon literature.

To the miners or other companions he had sometimes recited the verses that came to him, all of them lines throbbing with love for the Sierras, — for their vast forests and for their wild scenery, — or vibrating with sympathy for the oppressed Indians and every oppressed person.   In 1870 he published a volume of poetry, *Songs of the Sierras.* The novelty of his subjects attracted attention in England, and the book was so greatly admired that he went to London, where he was most kindly welcomed. *The Danites*, a play, *Memorie and Rime*— the fragments of a journal—and other works in prose, have appeared from his pen. He was, for a short time, a journalist in Washington, but finally returned to California, where he prefers living in retirement.

Walt Whitman, counting by his years (1819–1892), belongs both before and after the war. His main work was published several years before, but he did not come into notice until later. His style is so very, very singular, that it has been named Whitmanesque. His poetry lacks both meter and rhyme, and has long lines of any number of syllables. An example will give some idea of its peculiarities. His chief subject is *Myself:*

" Each man to himself, and each woman to herself, is
    the word of the past and present, and the true
    word of immortality ;
No one can acquire for another — not one,
No one can grow for another — not one.
The song is to the singer, and comes back most to him ;
The teaching is to the teacher, and comes back most
    to him ;
The murder is to the murderer, and comes back most
    to him."

Those who like Whitman's style—and several of England's famous critics are among them—say he is "the poet of the future," and that in the next century such a style will be very popular. Those who think his slang, his coarseness, his bad English, his lack of meter disgusting have wittily called admiration for him "Whitmania." He was a carpenter, building small houses and then selling them. Then he was editor of a small paper. Hospital nursing during the war ruined his health and he was partially paralyzed for years. His home was in Camden, New Jersey, and in his latter years he was partly dependent on his friends. *My Captain, O my Captain!* written on Lincoln's death, is singularly well done, and is liked by everybody. In this respect it is peculiar among Mr. Whitman's writings.

Dialect Poetry. — Bret Harte's dialect poetry was the first of its kind, but he has had many imitators — not of Rocky Mountain dialect, for no one else would like to follow him, but of the dialect of nearly every other section. Dialect is any form of speech peculiar to a particular part of the country and not agreeing with the ordinary rules of grammar. Nearly every part of the country has its own slang words, its own oddities of pronunciation, its own peculiar expressions. Bret Harte noticed the oddities of the miners' talk, and amused us with them. James Whitcomb Riley has noticed the oddities of the old-time "Hoosier" language in Indiana and its neighboring States, and is therefore known as "the Hoosier poet." His poetry is quite popular just now. Charles G. Leland, who is the author of many books on literary subjects, and is the best authority on the gypsies, has employed the German brogue most laughably in his *Hans Breitmann's Ballads.* "Hans Breitmann gif a barty" is the opening line of one of the funniest of the ballads.

Other Minor Poets. — Very popular are Will Carleton's city and country ballads. Is there a schoolhouse that has not echoed to the recitation of *The New Organ,* or of *Betsey and I are Out,* or of *Betsey and I are In?* John Hay, writer of a *Life of Lincoln,* is known for his *Pike County Ballads,* in which are the two poems *Jim Bludso* and *Little Breeches.*

A good many years ago a stock recitation was *Nothing to Wear*, by William Allen Butler; and Miss Flora McFlimsey, who had so many dresses she had nothing to wear, is a character known to everybody. John Godfrey Saxe was a humorous poet by profession, and a good humorous poet too. His lines fairly sparkle with fun and are plentifully sprinkled with puns. His works, it is said, have gone through forty editions, so pleasant is his fun. *Proud Miss McBride* and *Riding on the Rail* are specimens of his bright wit; and he has put in poetical and humorous form some of the old stories of mythology and of Greek and Roman history.

Summary.—Bret Harte (1838–   ), poet and story teller of the Rocky Mountains; born in Albany, but went to California when a boy. Edited *Overland Magazine;* came East in 1870; has lived much of the time in England. Stories: *The Luck of Roaring Camp, The Outcasts of Poker Flat, Miggles, Tennessee's Partner, How Santa Claus Came to Simpson's Bar, Tales of the Argonauts, Gabriel Conroy* (novel). Poems: *The Heathen Chinee, The Society upon the Stanislaus, Dow's Flat, The Greyport Legend.*

Joaquin Miller (1841–), "poet of the Sierras." His father moved to Oregon, where he became acquainted with pioneer life. He published his first volume in 1870. Poems: *Songs of the Sierras;* has written stories, sketches, and other volumes of poetry, as *Songs of the Sunlands.*

Walt Whitman (1819–92), born on Long Island; most peculiar poet in style, writes without meter. Chief work: *Leaves of Grass; November Boughs* is another. Best single piece, *My Captain, O my Captain!*

Dialect and Humorous Poets: James Whitcomb Riley,
"the Hoosier poet," writes in Hoosier dialect.
Will Carleton, *Farm Ballads* and *City Ballads*,
six volumes in all; best single poems: *Betsey
and I are Out, The New Organ.* Charles G.
Leland, prose author of merit, wrote *Hans Breit-
mann's Ballads.* John Godfrey Saxe (1816–87),
humorous poet, very popular; *Proud Miss
McBride, The Echo,* and *Riding on the Rail.*
John Hay wrote two poems well known: *Little
Breeches* and *Jim Bludso;* volume of poetry, *Pike
County Ballads;* a prose writer also. William
Allen Butler, author of the humorous satire
Nothing to Wear.

Quotations from Joaquin Miller.

O God! 'tis pitiful to see
  This miser so forlorn and old;
O God! how poor a man may be
  With nothing in this world but gold!

Is it worth while that we jostle a brother
  Bearing his load on the rough road of life?
Is it worth while that we jeer at each other
  In blackness of heart? — that we war to the knife?
    God pity us all in our pitiful strife!

OREGON.

Where the plants are as trees; where the trees are as
    towers
That toy, as it seems, with the stars of night.
Where white-flashing mountains flow rivers of yellow
  As a rock of the desert flowed fountains of old;

   .   .   .   .   .

Where the sun takes flame, and you wonder whether
  'Tis an isle of fire in his foamy bed;
Where the ends of the earth they are welding together
  In a rough-hewn fashion in a forge-flame red.

Here lifts the land of clouds ! The mantled forms,
   Made white with everlasting snow, look down
Through mists of many cañons, and the storms
   That stretch from Autumn time until they drown
   The yellow hem of Spring. The cedars frown
Dark brow'd through banner'd clouds that stretch and
     stream
   Above the sea from snowy mountain crown.
The heavens roll, and all things drift or seem
To drift about and drive like some majestic dream.

FOR THOSE WHO FAIL.

Oh, great is the hero who wins a name,
   But greater many and many a time
Some pale-faced fellow who dies in shame,
   And lets God finish the thought sublime.
            MEMORIE AND RIME.

From Walt Whitman.

Great is Youth — equally great is Old Age — great are
   Day and Night.
Great is Wealth — great is Poverty — great is Expres-
   sion — great is Silence.

What am I after all but a child pleas'd with the sound of
   my own name? repeating it over and over
I stand apart to hear — it never tires me.

      I loaf and invite my soul,
I lean and loaf at my ease, observing a spear of summer
   grass.

   .   .   .   .   .

I guess it must be the flag of my disposition out of hopeful green stuff woven —

   .   .   .   .   .

A scented gift and remembrance designedly dropt,
Bearing the owner's name someway in the corners, that
   we may see and remark and say " Whose ? "
            SONG OF MYSELF.

A Specimen of Riley's Hoosier Poetry.

Folks in town, I reckon, thinks
    They git all the fun they air
Runnin' loose 'round ! — but, 'y jinks !
    We got fun and fun to spare
Right out here amongst the ash
    And oak timber ever'where !
Some folks else kin cut a dash
    'Sides town people, don't fergit ! —
'Specially in winter time,
    When they's snow and roads is fit.
In them circumstances I'm
    Resignated to my lot —
Which puts me in mind o' what
'S called " The Literary."

A few Specimen Lines from Carleton.

It isn't a scrumptious thing to see —
    It's rather short of paint —
Its brow will al'ays wrinkled be;
    Its tick is growin' faint;
The circulation's noways good —
    The jints too stiffly play —
It some'at of'ner than it should
    Forgits the time of day;
'Twill stop an' try to recollect
    Fur somethin' like a week:
But there'd be music, I suspect,
    If our ol' clock could speak !

If to trace a hidden sorrow were within the doctor's art,
They ha' found a mortgage lying on that woman's broken
    heart.
Worm or beetle, drouth or tempest, on a farmer's land
    may fall,
But for first-class ruination trust a mortgage 'gainst them
    all.

From Leland.

Hans Breitmann gif a barty,
Dey had biano-blayin;

I felled in love mit a Merican frau,
Her name was Madilda Yane.
She had haar as prown ash a pretzel,
Her eyes vas himmel-plue,
And ven dey looket indo mine,
Dey shplit mine heart in two.

From Saxe.

Of all the notable things on earth
The queerest one is pride of birth
  Among our fierce democracy.
A bridge across a hundred years,
Without a prop to save it from sneers,
Not even a couple of rotten *peers*, —
A thing for laughter, fleers, and jeers,
  Is American aristocracy !

  Singing through the forests,
  Rattling over ridges;

  .   .   .   .

  Bless me ! this is pleasant,
  Riding on the rail !
  Men of different *stations*,
    In the eye of fame,
  Here are very quickly
    Coming to the same ;
  High and lowly people,
    Birds of every feather,
  On a common level
    Traveling together.

I asked of Echo, t'other day
  (Whose words are few and often funny),
What to a novice she could say
  Of courtship, love, and matrimony.
  Quoth Echo plainly, — "Matter-o'-money !"

  But learn to wear a sober phiz,
    Be stupid if you can :
  It's such a very serious thing
    To be a funny man.

CHAPTER XXIII.

Of a very different type from the groups of the last chapter is our group of critic and editor poets: Stedman, Stoddard, Aldrich, and Gilder. A delightful way of becoming acquainted with an author is to read his writings in connection with criticisms on them from Stedman or Stoddard : it is like having the guidance of an inspiring teacher.

Edmund Clarence Stedman had a college training at Yale, and early began the duties of an editor. He afterwards took up a business life that he might have time and means to afford the luxury of writing poetry. He is a banker on Wall Street, and his home is a literary center where young writers find help and encouragement. He has delivered lectures on poetry, has contributed articles to our magazines on different poets, and has done us good service by his books, *Poets of America* and *Victorian Poets*. The latter contains criticisms on the English poets of Queen Victoria's reign. Some of his own poems are *Pan in Wall Street*, *The Diamond Wedding*, *How Old John Brown Took Harper's Ferry*, and *Rip Van Winkle and his Wonderful Nap*. The youngest child can understand *What the Winds Bring:*

" Which is the wind that brings the cold ?
The north wind, Freddy, and all the snow."

Very simple also is the little love scene described in *The Doorstep* — the young boy escorting home the young girl after preaching, and the kiss on the door-step:

> " Perhaps 'twas boyish love, yet still
>
> .   .   .   .
>
> To feel once more that fresh wild thrill
> I'd give —   But who can live youth over?"

Richard Henry Stoddard. — Side by side with Stedman in knowledge of both modern and classic poetry stands Richard Henry Stoddard, who, in his criticisms, seems to possess "almost infallible judgment." Stoddard is a living lesson before every American boy of the possibilities in reach of perseverance and ambition. His sea-captain father having died, his widowed mother moved to New York in the hope of finding work to support her family. "A very foolish move," her son says, "for if she was poor in the country among relatives and friends, what would she be in a city among strangers!"

The boy sold matches, was office boy, a drudge under a tailor, a blacksmith's apprentice, and after he was fully grown he worked as an iron molder in a foundry. Whatever he was doing, the hard work did not drive away his longing for knowledge nor his love of poetry, and he spent his nights studying and composing verses. He has told us of his first discovery of a real piece of poetry. Before he moved to New York a copy of Watts's *Hymns* was the only poetry he had ever seen. One day while studying his reading lesson for school he came across a piece that he knew was not prose, because it was lined, and it was about a country pleasure which Richard had enjoyed — sliding down the hay in the barn. He recognized the ring: it was all there — the run

across the floor, the climbing the mow, the swift
rush downwards. The poem awoke in him a love
of poetry. He never forgot his debt to the writer
of the piece, N. P. Willis; and afterwards Willis was
very kind to him, encouraging him by his criticisms.
From the foundry young Stoddard went into the custom house, and finally he became literary reviewer
for the *Mail and Express*. He, too, is a lecturer,
and he, too, has done good service by such books
as *The Late English Poets* and *The Loves and Heroines
of the Poets*. His own ballads are stirring. His blank
verse is fine, and often treats of common things; but
his imagination makes these things beautiful. *The
Dead Master* and *Hymns to the Sea* are two of his
poetical productions. Best known of his single poems
is *It Never Comes Again* — that which "never comes
again" being the something which youth, departing,
takes from our hearts; for

> " Something beautiful is vanished,
>   .   .   .   .
> And will never come again."

In another tiny poem he tells of " how his songs are
wrought," that :

> " Like the blowing of the wind,
>   Or the flowing of the stream,
> Is the music in my mind."

His wife, who is also a poet, has written two or three
novels of New England life.

Thomas Bailey Aldrich is one who plays all
kinds of practical jokes in his stories, for he is a
story teller as well as a poet. *Marjorie Daw* is a
trap into which every reader walks unsuspectingly.
Like all the quizzing games in which the fun consists

in mystifying the one to be initiated, the fun is spoiled if you know beforehand — you must read the story yourself. His *Story of a Bad Boy* is very entertaining, for the boy, Aldrich himself, is not very bad, only mischief loving. His longer romances are *Prudence Palfrey*, *The Queen of Sheba*, and *The Stillwater Tragedy*. He is a dainty, polished poet, every line of his verse fitting exquisitely into another. His originality gives clever unexpected turns to his sentences as well as to his stories. He is popular in both France and Germany through translations. *Babie Bell* is one of his earlier poetical gems which met with instant favor. *The Face against the Pane* is another of his pieces, and *Before and After the Rain*. He writes particularly good society verses, and often epigrams of just a few lines, full of point. *Cloth of Gold*, *Flower and Thorn*, are two of his volumes of poetry. While editor of the *Atlantic Monthly* he did some of his best work.

Richard Watson Gilder. — Another editor, one who has done a great deal for American literature through the influence of his magazine, is Richard Watson Gilder, of the *Century*. He was associated with Holland when that periodical was called *Scribner's Monthly*, and since Holland's death he has had charge of the editorship himself. He is by birth and training peculiarly fitted for his position. His father, a Methodist preacher, was editor of two papers, and loved to write; his children resembled him, and there are three editors among them. Gilder was such a frail, delicate child that he went to school only one day, his father teaching him at home thereafter. One day going with his father to the office of some newspaper, the editor placed the young visitor on a soap box and showed him how to set type. He was delighted. Instead of marbles and tops he began carrying type in his pockets. At twelve he was editing, printing, and publishing a little newspaper; at sixteen he and two other lads were publishing a campaign paper. The death of his father compelled him to give up the study of law and to get into a business of some kind. The first business that offered itself was the position of paymaster on a railroad, but his wish was to be a writer. He gladly became a reporter, rising after a time to the position of editor. Starting a paper of his own, he strained every nerve to make it succeed, undertaking at the same time the editorship of another paper, and working day and night. The Poets' Corner of the papers now and then had a sonnet or an epigram from him. The best known is his *Sonnet* on a sonnet:

> " What is a sonnet? 'Tis a pearly shell
>   That murmurs of the far-off murmuring sea."

His duties on the *Century* do not keep him from poetry. He not only writes polished poems, but there is height and depth to some of them. *The New Day* and *The Poet and the Master* contain many of his best pieces. Isn't there love in these lines ? —

> " I count my time by times that I meet thee :
>   .   .   .   .   .
> Slow fly the hours, fast the hours flee,
> If thou art far from, or art near to me.
>   .   .   .   .   ..
> Thou art my dream come true, and thou my dream,
> The air I breathe, the world wherein I dwell," etc.

Sidney Lanier. — In a lecture delivered in 1893, the president of Amherst College says of a poet and critic who has passed away from earth : " Beyond any other poet he shows a love for plant life and trees. Again, he was preëminently a musician in his art.

. . . His was a trained mind; . . . his volumes of prose are invaluable for students; . . . and a rapidly increasing number of young people are consulting his works for inspiration and guidance. . . . His wealth of imagination, . . . his union of close study and broad reading with deep poetic insight— . . . all these mark him as a *great* poet." The one of whom these words are spoken is Sidney Lanier, first in rank of the Southern group of poets.

The story of his life is sad enough for tears, for his manhood years were spent in an unequal battle against disease and poverty, and he fell in the battle just as he had "conquered success" and the world was beginning to realize that a genius was among us. After being graduated at college with first honors he was made tutor in the same institution, but was one of the first volunteer soldiers of the Confederacy. He came out from a war prison with consumption, but the necessity of earning a living was before him. He tried clerking and teaching. Then he tried law, but he longed for more knowledge and a literary life —both seemingly impossible in the impoverished South. One thing was a passion with him—music. When a little boy he had begun practicing on the flute; he had carried it all through the war, and was, perhaps, one of the finest performers in America. He played "first flute" in Baltimore concerts, thus earning a meager support for his family, while at the public library he read and studied like a famished man. His poems finally began to be praised. At the opening of the Centennial a cantata by him was sung, and in 1879 he was asked to deliver lectures on literature at Johns Hopkins University, Baltimore. He was then in the last stages of consumption, and it was wonderful that he could go through with the task. In two years he was dead. Since his death his poetry has been collected into a volume, and his critical prose works, *The English Novel* and *The Science of English Verse*, have been published. *The Boys' King Arthur* and similar books tell for young people the legends of King Arthur and his Round Table, the history or chronicles of Froissart, and the ancient legends of Wales. He had a literary gift in criticism. His poetry is not like any other poetry. Critics complain that he tried to use new and strange terms and unusual words. His admirers think that he would soon have overcome this fault, or that perhaps he would have educated others to his style. All acknowledge his talent. He is intensely musical, and his thoughts are noble and true.

His Poems. — *The Marshes of Glynn, Corn, Sunrise, The Song of the Chattahoochee*, are full of Nature. Very sweet are the love lines to his wife's eyes, *My Springs*. It is said that she, too, was devoted to books, and when there was not enough money for both the longed-for book and some coal, the book would generally be bought, and they would sit together over the cold register and forget the weather in the pleasure of reading. Of her eyes he sings that when Love, Faith, Hope, all had fled, he would look in those his "two springs" and find a charm that would bring them back to him:

> " Dear eyes, dear eyes, and rare, complete, —
> Being heavenly sweet and earthly sweet, —
> I wonder that God made you mine,
> For when He frowns, 'tis then ye shine ! "

The laureate of South Carolina is Paul Hamilton Hayne. Born in Charleston in 1830, of a famous and wealthy family, he had literary advantages, and began versemaking early, being greatly influenced by Simms. He edited a Southern magazine and did much good by it, for no Southerner strove harder to help his own country by literature. Before the war a volume of his poems won favor. The war changed all. He went into the army, gained distinction by his bravery, and came forth poor, his home being gone. In the pine barrens near Augusta, Georgia, he built a little cottage, and there tried to gain a support and recover his broken health. For twenty years he kept up the struggle, dying in 1886. He is a lyric poet. Some of his battle lyrics are trumpet peals, but his quiet pieces are soft and lovely. Always he calls to courage and action :

> " 'Tis the part of a coward to brood
>   Over a past that is withered and dead."

Exultantly, when he knew himself on the verge of the grave, does he sing in *Face to Face:*

> " Sad mortal, wouldst thou but know
>   What truly it is to die,
>   The wings of thy soul would glow,
>   And the hopes of thy heart beat high ! "

He, too, has poured out a love song to his wife, *Love's Autumn.* In his *Life of Timrod* we see much of his heart. Timrod was a gentle poet who died before he had given much more than a promise of future fame. *Earth's Odors after Rain, The Battle of King's Mountain,* and *The Pine's Mystery* are some of Hayne's poems. His son, William Hamilton Hayne, is a poet.

Maurice Thompson.—Georgia likes to claim Maurice Thompson, critic, essayist, and poet, as her son, for, though born in Indiana, he was taken when a child to Georgia. But his summer home is again in Indiana. *Sylvan Secrets, Songs of Fair Weather, Byways and Birdnotes,* are appropriate names for his books, for he is a lover of " outdoors." The most accomplished living archer and a splendid shot, he makes long excursions, bringing back in his hands pencil pictures of what he has seen, and in his brain word pictures. A few years ago he was made chief of the department of geology in Indiana.

America can claim the Irish poet and patriot, John Boyle O'Reilly, who became editor of the *Boston Pilot. Songs of the Southern Seas*, and *The Statues in the Block*, are two volumes of his poems.

Summary.—NORTHERN GROUP: Edmund Clarence Stedman (1833–   ). Works on Criticism : *The Victorian Poets* and *Poets of America.* Poems : *Pan in Wall Street, The Diamond Wedding, Gettysburg, Hawthorne, The Doorstep.*

Richard Henry Stoddard (1825–   ). Books of Criticism : *The Late English Poets* and *Loves and Heroines of the Poets.* Poems : *The Dead Master, Hymns to the Sea, The King's Bell, Songs of Summer, The Book of the East.*

Thomas Bailey Aldrich (1836–   ). Stories : *Marjorie Daw, and other Stories, Story of a Bad Boy, Prudence Palfrey, Queen of Sheba, Stillwater Tragedy.* Volumes of Poetry : *Cloth of Gold* and *Flower and Thorn.* Single Poems : *Babie Bell, The Face against the Pane, Before and After the Rain.*

Richard Watson Gilder (1844–   ). Poems : *The New Day, The Celestial Passion.*

SOUTHERN GROUP : Sidney Lanier (1842–81), Georgia, critic. Lecturer on literature at Johns Hopkins. Prose Works : *Tiger Lilies* (novel), *The Science of English Verse, The English Novel,* and several books for boys. Poems (one volume published after his death) : *The Marshes of Glynn, Sunrise, Corn, The Song of the Chattahoochee.*

Paul Hamilton Hayne (1830–86), South Carolina, lyric poet.   Poems: *Preëxistence, The Battle of King's Mountain, The Pine's Mystery, Face to Face, Love's Autumn, Earth's Odors after Rain.*

Henry Timrod (1829–67), South Carolina.   *A Mother's Wail, Spring.*

Maurice Thompson (1844–   ). Books: *Songs of Fair Weather, Sylvan Secrets, Byways and Birdnotes.*

IRISH POET AND JOURNALIST: John Boyle O'Reilly (1844–90).   Books: *Songs of Southern Seas, The Statues in the Block.*

From Stedman.

No past the glad heart cowers,
    No memories dark:
Only the sunny hours,
    The dial mark.

Not so much nearer wisdom is a man than a boy forsooth,
Though, in scorn of what has come and gone, he hates
    the ways of youth.

From Stoddard.

There are gains for all our losses,
    There are balms for all our pain;
But when youth, the dream, departs,
It takes something from our hearts,
    And it never comes again.

We hold the keys of heaven within our hands,
    The gift and heirloom of a former state,
    And lie in infancy at heaven's gate,
Transfigured in the light that streams along the lands!
Around our pillows golden ladders rise,
And up and down the skies,
With wingèd sandals shod,
The angels come and go, the Messengers of God!

Not what we would, but what we must,
Makes up the sum of living ; . . .
Swords cleave to hands that sought the plow,
And laurels miss the soldier's brow.

From Aldrich.

Hypatia — ah, what lovely things
Are fashioned out of eighteen springs !

We knew it would rain, for all the morn
    A spirit on slender ropes of mist
Was lowering its golden buckets down
    Into the vapory amethyst

Of marshes and swamps and dismal fens, —
    Scooping the dew that lay in the flowers,
Dipping the jewels out of the sea,
    To sprinkle them over the land in showers.

Sorrow itself is not so hard to bear as the thought of
sorrow coming. Airy ghosts that work no harm do ter-
rify us more than men in steel with bloody purposes.
A wide-spreading, hopeful disposition is your only true
umbrella in this vale of tears.

From Gilder.

Not from the whole wide world I chose thee —
Sweetheart, light of the land and the sea !
The wide, wide world could not inclose thee,
For thou art the whole wide world to me.

Each moment holy is, for out from God
Each moment flashes forth a human soul.
Holy each moment is, for back to him
Some wandering soul each moment home returns.

Now you who rhyme, and I who rhyme,
Have not we sworn it many a time,
That we no more our verse would scrawl,
For Shakespeare he had said it all !

Wherever are tears and sighs,
Wherever are children's eyes,
Where man calls man his brother
And loves as himself another,
    Christ lives!

Love, Love, my Love:
  The best things are the truest!
When the earth lies shadowy dark below,
  Oh, then the heavens are bluest!

From Lanier.

O Love! O Wife! thine eyes are they, —
My springs from out whose shining gray
Issue the sweet celestial streams
That feed my life's bright Lake of Dreams.

Oval and large and passion-pure,
And gray and wise and honor-sure;
Soft as a dying violet breath,
Yet calmly unafraid of death.

As the marsh hen secretly builds on the watery sod,
Behold, I will build me a nest on the greatness of God!
I will fly in the greatness of God as the marsh hen flies
In the freedom that fills all the space 'twixt the marsh and
    the skies.

By so many roots as the marsh grass sends in the sod,
I will heartily lay me ahold of the greatness of God.

From Hayne.

But I, earth's madness above,
  In a kingdom of stormless breath —
I gaze on the glory of love
  In the unveiled face of Death.

And from heaven of heavens above
  God speaketh with bateless breath —
My angel of perfect love
  Is the angel men call Death!

From Timrod.

Spring, with that nameless pathos in the air
Which dwells in all things fair, —
Spring, with her golden suns and silver rain,
Is with us once again.

In the deep heart of every forest tree
The blood is all aglee,
And there's a look about the leafless bowers
As if they dreamed of flowers.

He wields the deadliest blade of all
Who lightest holds his life.

From Thompson.

He is a poet strong and true
Who loves wild thyme and honey dew;
And like a brown bee works and sings,
With morning freshness on his wings,
And a gold burden on his thighs:
The pollen-dust of centuries.

Short is his song, but strangely sweet
To ears aweary of the low,
Dull tramp of Winter's sullen feet,
Sandaled in ice and muffled in snow.

From O'Reilly.

How shall I a habit break?
As you did that habit make.
As you gathered, you must lose,
As you yielded, now refuse.
Thread by thread the strands we twist
Till they bind us, neck and wrist.
Thread by thread the patient hand
Must untwine ere free we stand.

CHAPTER XXIV.

"AND WOMEN SINGERS."

The Cary Sisters. — No creative genius has arisen among American women, but there have been many whose songs have brightened and sweetened the lives of others, many who are held dear in the hearts of readers. Before the war were the two sisters, Alice and Phœbe Cary. *Pictures of Memory* recalls to us Alice, and the oft-quoted words, " It is only noble to be good," give the moral that flows through all her verses, for they are home sermons, as are her prose works. Though Phœbe's special charm in conversation was her sparkling wit, her name lives now for the hymn, *One Sweetly Solemn Thought.* One died in 1870, the other a year later.

Helen Hunt Jackson. — The most distinguished of our woman poets — distinguished for her stories, distinguished for what she has done — is Helen Hunt Jackson, known by her pen name, " H. H." The daughter of Professor Fiske, she was a charming girl in society, very bright, but with no ambition to be a writer. Even after her marriage to Major Hunt, a talented naval engineer, she devoted her time to the duties of a wife and mother, and the demands of society. Her husband was killed while experimenting with one of his own submarine inventions, and not long afterwards her only child, a son " of remarkable promise," died. Like fragrant flowers when bruised, her crushed, broken heart poured forth its sweetness — sweetness that has soothed other broken hearts — in deep, spiritual poems.   When collected in a volume she called them by the single title, *Verses.* *My Heritage*, *Burnt Ships*, and *At Last* are three of her poems.   On a trip to Europe she wrote back such delightful letters, so full of good humor and grace, that a friend persuaded her to print them in a book entitled *Bits of Travel.*   Four other *Bits* followed; one is *Bits of Talk for Young Folks.*   Though she never acknowledged it, it is believed that the two novels, *Mercy Philbrick's Choice* and *Hetty's Strange History*, were written by her.

Her Work for the Indians. — Severe attacks of diphtheria drove her from the literary society of Newport to Colorado, where she married Mr. Jackson and became interested in that cause now identified with her name, the cause of the Indians.   From 1880 to 1885, the year of her death, her heart, mind, and pen were devoted to this one subject.   Her *Century of Dishonor*, showing the dishonor of our dealings with the Indians, caused her to be appointed by the United States Government to examine into the needs of the California Indians.   She was the first woman ever appointed to such a place.   *Ramona*, a story, is another appeal for the red race ; and "these," she declared, "are the only things I have done of which I am glad now."   Well she might be glad of them, for the two works changed the feelings of many people towards the Indians, and brought in juster measures.   Both books give the truth and the real facts notwithstanding the story form of *Ramona*.   She thought of writing a child's story on the same theme, and her other stories for children, as *Nelly's Silver Mine* and her tales about *Cats*, make us wish she had carried out the thought.   Every year adds new names to the list of her readers and admirers.   *Ramona* is

one of those fascinatingly pathetic books which appeal
to young people's sympathies and absorb them with
their interest.

Her " Best " is a little poem that has comforted
other mothers who have lost their little ones. The
bereaved mother in it can feel the joy to which her
child has gone, and know and say,

> "And that is best."

It seems to us that no woman's life was much fuller
of labor for others and of helpful good than was
Helen Hunt Jackson's, and yet the last lines that she
ever wrote are deeply humble:

> " Father, I scarcely dare to pray,
>   Too clear I see, now it is done,
> That I have wasted half my day
>   And left my work but just begun.
>
>   .   .   .   .
>
> Too clear I see that I have sought,
>   Unconscious, selfish aims to win."

" A Daughter of Israel." — What Mrs. Jackson
tried to do for one downtrodden nation not her own,
Emma Lazarus tried to do for her own Hebrew race.
From her childhood she showed intense depth of
feeling and unusual brain power; but there was a
sadness about her writings, and, I think, in her
own feelings, when she wrote poetry, or made translations from other languages, or restlessly sought for the
something to satisfy her. Some of Emerson's inspiring thoughts stimulated her heart and mind, and his
personal friendship and advice helped her. In 1879
a cruel persecution of the Jews was begun in different
parts of Europe. Up to this time her poetry had

been lofty in tone, but modeled after Greek and German poets, with no reference to her own people, for she seemed almost indifferent to her blood and faith. Now she turned from the study of Greek and German literature, and from the translation of Heine, the German poet, to the literature and religion of the Hebrews. Her one passionate idea was that Israel should again be a nation and live in Canaan. In prose and poetry she earnestly espoused the cause of her people, rousing them and others by such lyrics as *The Banner of the Jew*, *The New Ezekiel*, and *By the Waters of Babylon*, all found in her *Songs of a Semite*. Her most striking work is *The Dance to Death*, a drama representing the persecution of the Jews in the twelfth century. The line,

> "I am all Israel's now,"

certainly applied to herself. With all her fervor and enthusiasm, her simplicity and modesty were wonderful, nor was she spoiled by the honors which she received. Her last years were years of suffering, during which she wrote but little. When she died in 1887, aged only thirty-eight, it was felt that a poet of perhaps high rank had passed from among us.

Many other names can be mentioned: Celia Thaxter, Lucy Larcom, Nora Perry, Rose Terry Cooke, Margaret Preston, Edith Thomas, Margaret E. Sangster, Sarah Woolsey (Susan Coolidge), Margaret Deland, the Goodale sisters. It is difficult among so large a number to select, and still more difficult to omit.

Celia Thaxter succeeded in catching the spirit of the ocean in her two books of poems, *Among the Isles of Shoals* and *Drift Wood*. This is no wonder, however, for her home was a lighthouse, where her father, though a gentleman and scholar, had retired and be-

come the keeper. As a child, shells, rocks, and waves
were her playthings, Shakespeare her only story book,
and Nature her teacher. Her verses and pure descriptions of the place have made the Isles of Shoals (off
New Hampshire) a favorite visiting place for tourists.
The Sandpiper is one of her trustful songs. *Poems for
Children* is another popular volume by her.

Lucy Larcom loved the mountains as much as
Celia Thaxter loved the sea. She was a self-made
woman. When a mill hand in Lowell, Massachusetts,
she started among the mill girls a little paper. Whittier
saw her poetry and encouraged her, forming with
her a sacred friendship. Being forbidden to read
books in the mill, she pasted on her window sill newspaper scraps of favorite poems, and these she learned
by heart. At last she had an opportunity to go to
school, and after she was graduated she taught eight
years in a seminary. Then for a time she edited
Our Young Folks. She knew Nature and loved both
Nature and God, and she sang of both in song and
hymn. *Childhood Songs* and *Wild Roses from Cape
Ann* are two of her volumes. *Hannah Binding Shoes*
is her best-known piece.

Other Writers. — Margaret Preston, of Virginia,
finds a place in such magazines as the *Century.* Her
poems are chiefly religious. Edith Thomas, a native
of Ohio, does exquisitely polished work. Margaret
Deland, of Boston, wrote *The Old Garden*, and has
written some successful novels also. Nora Perry and
Rose Terry Cooke are true to life in their story poems.
The Goodale sisters, Dora and Elaine, show simplicity in their verses.

Summary. — Alice Cary (1820–70), *Pictures of
Memory.* Phœbe Cary (1824–71), *Nearer Home.*
Helen Hunt Jackson (1831–85), Massachu-

setts, story writer as well as poet; *Verses, Bits of Travel,* several novels, and stories for children; *A Century of Dishonor* and *Ramona* (her best), written in interest of Indians.

Emma Lazarus (1849–87), New York, a Hebrew; *Songs of a Semite.*

Celia Thaxter (1836–94), New Hampshire; wrote of the sea; *The Isles of Shoals* and *Drift Wood,* volumes; *The Sandpiper* and *Before Sunrise,* single poems.

Lucy Larcom (1826–93), Massachusetts; from mill hand rose to be teacher, editor, poet; *Childhood Songs, Wild Roses from Cape Ann,* collections of her poems.

Margaret Preston, of Virginia; *Cartoons.*

Edith Thomas, of Ohio; *The Inverted Torch, In Sunshine Land* (for children).

Margaret Deland, of Pennsylvania, now of Boston; *The Old Garden,* and novels.

Nora Perry (died 1893); *After the Ball, and other Poems.*

Rose Terry Cooke (1827–92); *Poems.*

Elaine Goodale (Eastman) and Dora Goodale, Massachusetts; *Apple Blossoms, All Round the Year.*

A few Lines from Our Women Singers.
Alice Cary.

Do not look for wrong and evil:
   You will find them if you do.
As you measure for your neighbor,
   He will measure back to you.

Look for goodness, look for gladness:
   You will meet them all the while.
If you bring a smiling visage
   To the glass you meet a smile.

There is nothing more kingly than kindness,
There is nothing more royal than truth.

Phœbe Cary.

Sometimes, I think, the things we see
Are shadows of the things to be;
    That what we plan we build;
That every hope that hath been crossed,
And every dream we thought was lost,
    In heaven shall be fulfilled;

That even the children of the brain
Have not been born and died in vain,
    Though here unclothed and dumb;
But on some brighter, better shore
They live, embodied evermore,
    And wait for us to come.
                    DREAMS AND REALITIES.

Helen Hunt Jackson (H. H.).

All days are birthdays in the life,
    The blessed life that poets live.
Songs keep their own sweet festivals,
    And are the gifts they come to give.
The only triumph over Time,
    That Time permits, is his who sings;
The poet Time himself defies
    By secret help of Time's own wings.
TO HOLMES, ON HIS SEVENTIETH BIRTHDAY.

Find me the men on earth who care
    Enough for faith or creed to-day
To seek a barren wilderness
    For simple liberty to pray.

Despise their narrow creed who will!
    Pity their poverty who dare!
Their lives knew joys, their lives wore crowns,
    We do not know, we cannot wear.
                    FOREFATHERS' DAY.

Like a blind spinner in the sun,
    I tread my days.
I know that all the threads will run
    Appointed ways.
I know each day will bring its task,
And, being blind, no more I ask.

Emma Lazarus.

"Oh, World-God, give me Wealth!" the Egyptian
    cried.
His prayer was granted. . . .
Seek Pharaoh's race to-day and ye shall find
Rust and the moth, silence and dusty sleep.

"Oh, World-God, give me Beauty!" cried the Greek.
His prayer was granted. . . .
Go seek the sunshine race, ye find to-day
A broken column and a lute unstrung.

"Oh, World-God, give me Power!" the Roman cried.
His prayer was granted. . . .
A roofless ruin stands where once abode
The imperial race of everlasting Rome.

"Oh, Godhead, give me Truth!" the Hebrew cried.
His prayer was granted. . . .
No fire consumes him, neither floods devour —
Immortal through the lamp within his hand.

                                            GIFTS.

Celia Thaxter.

Buttercup nodded and said "Good-by;"
    Clover and daisy went off together;
But the fragrant water-lilies lie
    Yet moored in the golden August weather.

Dear little head, that lies in calm content
    Within the gracious hollow that God made
In every human shoulder, where He meant
    Some tired head for comfort should be laid.

                                            SONG.

Lucy Larcom.

Hand in hand with angels
 Through the world we go;
Brighter eyes are on us
 Than we blind ones know;
Tenderer voices cheer us
 Than we deaf will own:
Never, walking heavenward,
 Can we walk alone.

She likens prayers and hymns unto a stream
Flowing amid the sandy wastes of life,
Watering the roots of action; nerving up
The earnest toiler's strength.
      LEGEND OF A VEIL.

Doors hast thou opened for us, thinker, seer!
Bars let down into pastures measureless;
The air we breathe to-day, through thee, is freer
Than, buoyant with its freshness, we can guess.
        TO EMERSON.

Margaret Preston.

He loved the lilies; He made them fair;
 And sweet as the sweetest incense flows
The stream of its fragrance when I wear
 For Him, on my heart, a rose.
And, Father, I doubt not, there may hide
 Beneath the tatters thou bid'st me view
As much of arrogance, scorn, and pride
 As ever the ermine knew!

A spring upon whose brink the anemones
And hooded violets and shrinking ferns
And tremulous woodland things crowd unafraid,
Sure of the refreshing that they always find.

When a whole continent thrilled at Whittier's call;
Or smiled, delighted, o'er the wondrous "Shay;"
Or heard "The Raven" croak, . . .
What need to ask, "Have we a Poet here?"
      AMERICA'S POETS.

CHAPTER XXV.

SOME NOVELISTS OF THE DAY.

As has been said in a former chapter, readers and writers of novels have increased more than any other class of readers and writers. Hence it is very hard to make any selection among those who entertain us by fiction; it is hard to tell whose books will be read twenty or even ten years from now, and whose will be forgotten. But some of the most prominent writers, those whose names are constantly appearing in the magazines, may be remembered. The two who now stand at the head of the new schools of realistic and analytic fiction are William Dean Howells and Henry James.

William Dean Howells is now publishing his autobiography, and has told us much about himself in the half-true *A Boy's Town*. This town is Hamilton, Ohio, whither his father moved when William was a child of four. The boy early learned to work, and when he was twelve he set type in his father's printing office until late at night, and was up early in the morning distributing the papers. Such training did him good, and he learned more at home in books than at school. Our novelist took to reporting and writing poetry before he wrote stories, and at the same time picked up some Latin, Greek, Italian, French, and German. He wrote a campaign life of Lincoln when Lincoln was running for the

Presidency, and after the election he was made consul to Venice. He studied Italian life, language, and
literature thoroughly, and told of his experiences in
Italian Journeys and *Venetian Life*, which are said
to be as good as a guide book to visitors in Italy.
Their Wedding Journey describes a bridal tour through
New York; *A Chance Acquaintance*, a trip through
Canada. From these travels with a little story inter-
woven, he has gone on to real novel writing, sending
novels forth at the rate of one or two a year. He
was for some years the editor of the *Atlantic Monthly*.
Howells puts both sense and truth in every story,
and he gives real men and women — ordinary, every-
day men and women in ordinary situations. He will
be always more read by highly cultured people than
by average people, for he has not enough adventure
and excitement, and his characters are not romantic
enough to get his readers deeply interested in them.

" **A Woman's Reason** " is a story which every
girl ought to read, for it has helped American girls
to consider the duty of learning something — some
one thing — so well that it can be depended upon for
a support, if a support is needed. Howells's farces
are very bright. *The Mouse Trap* has been acted at
exhibitions and entertainments all over the United
States. He has also written some stories for children.

Henry James, son of a writer of the same name,
has spent so much of his life abroad that he is almost
as much a European as an American. He was born
in New York, but went to Europe when a youth to
finish his education, which was under tutors. His
favorite plot is one in which Americans and foreigners are contrasted. In *Daisy Miller* the heroine is
a wild American girl abroad. The story was much
read, much talked about, and not much liked by our
girls, who declared that it was not "fair." *A Bundle*

of Letters is very good. *The Europeans, The American, The Bostonians*, are a few of his works. *French Poets and Novelists* proves him to be a good critic. He is called analytic because he analyzes his characters, showing how they think and feel. Thus he often gives up pages to a description of their thoughts and motives, making them talk far more than they act; and they talk very cleverly, for James is witty. The dialogues are far wittier than most real conversations are apt to be.

Another author who is counted as American, but who lives abroad, is F. Marion Crawford, son of an American sculptor. His own experiences have been romantic enough to furnish him with material for several novels without his having to draw on his imagination. He edited a paper in India and lives in Italy. The scene of his story, *Mr. Isaacs*, is laid in the former country, and that of most of his other novels, as the delightful *Roman Singer*, in the latter sunny land. *Saracinesca* and *Paul Patoff* are among his works. He is said to be more popular in Europe than any other American novelist.

Mrs. Barr and Mrs. Burnett. — If we have sent two to other lands, we have been repaid by our imported writers, for both Mrs. Barr and Mrs. Frances Hodgson Burnett were born in England. Mrs. Burnett's family came over to Tennessee when she was a child. She has told us about her childhood in *The One I Knew the Best of All.* When very small she loved to make up stories to herself. She picked wild grapes to procure enough money to pay the postage on her first two published stories. When in 1873 *Surly Tim's Trouble* was published in *Scribner's Monthly* her future was secure. *That Lass o' Lowrie's* is strong and sweet, and describes mining life in Lancashire, England. *A Fair Barbarian* is a very amusing account of a Western girl's visit to England. All these stories, however, fade before *Little Lord Fauntleroy*, that book so popular with children. *Sara Crewe* is another favorite with children, and *Little Saint Elizabeth*. Mrs. Barr's most popular work is *Jan Vedder's Wife*. She has also written *A Bow of Orange Ribbon* and many other stories.

Norway has let us have Hjalmar Hjorth Boyesen, who wrote stories of his own country, making their interest all the fresher to us. *Ilka on the Hilltop* is one of his novels. For boys he has written both short and continued stories. His poems, *Naughty Brier Rose* and *Thora*, are well known.

There lives in America now and writes for American papers an Anglo-Indian, that is, a man of English parentage, born in India. This is Rudyard Kipling, whose stories are like nobody else's, and he too has written for children in his *Jungle Book*.

Frank R. Stockton.—Another creator of a new style of story is Frank R. Stockton, and he has no imitators. He makes the most absurd people and the most absurd situations seem real and serious. From his boyhood his tastes have been literary ; and it was for a literary club to which he belonged that he wrote the *Ting-a-ling Tales*. His first appearance in print was in the *Riverside Magazine*. *Rudder Grange* set all the readers of the old *Scribner's Monthly* laughing, and he kept on writing for both the *Century* and *St. Nicholas*. By one short story, not more than five or six pages long, he made himself famous as the man who wrote *The Lady or the Tiger?* Indeed, he says he is tired of the very words, so many letters have come to him asking him about it, and at last he has told the public how he happened to write it. The plot is of the simplest: An Eastern king, barbarous and tyrannical, instead of going through a trial

with accused persons, requires them to open one
of two doors in the amphitheater.   Behind one is a
fierce tiger, behind the other a beautiful lady whom
the accused man must marry.   Thus it seemed left
to the gods to decide their fate.   The king's daughter loves a member of the court, and her love is
returned.   When the presumption of this courtier is
discovered he is condemned to the fearful choice.
He enters, and as he bows to the princess she, by a
slight gesture, indicates one of the doors.   Which
door was it ?   Which would hurt her worse: to see
her lover devoured by a tiger, or to see him married to another — another of whom she was already
jealous ?   That is just how Stockton ends the story,
by that tantalizing " Which ?"   *The Hundredth Man,
The Casting Away of Mrs. Lecks and Mrs. Aleshine,*
and *Squirrel Inn* are three of his longer stories.

Edward Everett Hale. — Another author who
has been annoyed with letters about one of his stories
is Edward Everett Hale, historian, novelist, orator,
preacher, and leader in all movements to help the
world.   He, too, though in an entirely different way,
makes impossible things seem real.   *The Man Without a Country* is the story that brought the deluge of
letters, for it awakened much interest.   It is an eloquent lesson on love for one's country.   An officer
in the army had been guilty of treasonable conduct,
and during his trial he cursed his country, the United
States.   The judge thereupon condemned him to be
kept for the rest of his life on some ship at sea ; no
book or newspaper about the United States should be
given him ; the name of the country must always be
torn out, and it should never be mentioned in his
presence.   That was all the punishment, and yet he
found it torture and disgrace.   Read and see what a
man's country is worth to him.

To do good to people around him has always been
Hale's aim.   He showed in early childhood a passion for writing.   His father was an editor, and the
lad could print as soon as he could read, and at
eleven was writing pieces.   *The Brick Moon* and *My
Double, and How He Undid Me*, are two impossible
but fascinating tales, the latter being intensely laugh-
able.   Mr. Hale has written a story for boys, and
many religious and educational articles.   His *Ten
Times One is Ten* suggested the idea of circles of ten
in the King's Daughters and Sons, whose silver crosses
with the initials I. H. N. flash from New York to New
Zealand.   In Europe his *In His Name* has helped
others; in the mountains of South America *The Man
Without a Country* has taught patriotism.   Such rewards satisfy our author better than if he had reached
the topmost place in literature.

Lewis Wallace is the author of *Ben-Hur: A Tale
of the Christ*, a book that was wonderfully popular a
short time ago.   His idle schooldays and his hard-
fighting soldier days in the Mexican and Civil Wars
did not lay a good literary foundation, and critics see
plainly this lack.   His numerous readers care little
for his slips in language, so thrilling is the interest of
Ben-Hur.   *The Fair God* is an historical novel re-
lating to the conquest of Mexico by Cortez.   *The
Prince of India* is his latest work.

Other Story Tellers. — If you read the magazines
you will become familiar with the names of Robert
Grant, Brander Matthews, Thomas A. Janvier, and
other prominent writers of to-day.   Julian Hawthorne,
son of the great novelist, has written some stories.
George Parsons Lathrop, who married Rose Hawthorne (also a poet and story writer), is a poet, novelist
and miscellaneous writer.   Yet with all these names
you probably miss names seen on the title-pages of

several popular novels.   Most of those omitted would
hurt your soul and weaken your mind if you read
nothing but their works.   A few will not harm your
heart and soul, though they will not make your brain
grow faster.   Such a one is the Rev. E. P. Roe, who
pleases the multitude and speaks bravely for the
right, but whose works are commonplace and without literary merit.

Summary.— NOVELISTS AND STORY TELLERS.
William Dean Howells (1837–   ), Ohio.   Began by
    writing verses; writes for leading magazines;
    was editor of *Atlantic Monthly* for years. Works:
    *A Modern Instance, A Woman's Reason, April
    Hopes, The Rise of Silas Lapham, A Hazard of
    New Fortunes, The World of Chance, Criticism
    and Fiction,* etc.   Farces: *The Mouse Trap, The
    Elevator,* etc.
Henry James (1843–   ), New York; has lived abroad
    a great deal; very analytic.   Works: *Daisy
    Miller, The Europeans, The American, The Bos-
    tonians.*   Criticism: *French Poets and Novelists.*
F. Marion Crawford (1845–   ), son of an American
    sculptor, lives in Italy; our most popular novel-
    ist abroad.   *A Roman Singer, Saracinesca, Mr.
    Isaacs, Katherine Lauderdale,* etc.
Frances Hodgson Burnett (1849–   ), England; *A
    Fair Barbarian, Haworths, That Lass o' Low-
    ries, The One I Knew the Best of All.*   For
    Children: *Little Lord Fauntleroy, Sara Crewe.*
Amelia Barr (1831–   ), born in England; home in
    New York State; *A Daughter of Fife, Jan Ved-
    der's Wife.*
Hjalmar Hjörth Boyesen (1848–1895), born in Nor-
    way; *Gunnar, Tales from Two Hemispheres,*
    poems; stories of Norwegian life, for children.

Rudyard Kipling (1865–   ), born in India, now living
in America, writes brilliant stories of India.   *The
Jungle Book*, for children.

Frank R. Stockton (1834–   ), born in Philadelphia,
lives in New Jersey; humorous and original.
Better in short stories; writes for children too.
Short Stories: *The Lady or The Tiger? Negative
Gravity.* Books: *Rudder Grange, The Hundredth
Man*, etc.

Edward Everett Hale (1822–   ), Boston; essayist,
lecturer, historian, religious writer, active in re-
forms.   Short Stories: *The Man Without a
Country, My Double, and How He Undid Me,
If, Yes, and Perhaps.* Books: *In His Name,
Ten Times One is Ten*, etc.

Lewis Wallace (1827–   ), Indiana; statesman and
soldier; *Ben-Hur: A Tale of the Christ, The
Fair God, The Prince of India.*

Edward Payson Roe (1838–87), very commonplace,
but popular; *Barriers Burned Away, From Jest
to Earnest*, etc.   Wrote also a horticultural book,
Success with Small Fruits.

Julian Hawthorne (1846–   ), born in Boston, now
living in Jamaica; has written stories and criticisms for the magazines, also a biography of
Nathaniel Hawthorne and his Wife, and several
novels.

George Parsons Lathrop (1851–   ), born in Hono-
lulu, poet and story writer; *Rose and Roof Tree*
(poems), *An Echo of Passion* (novel).

Other writers: Robert Grant, Brander Matthews,
Thomas A. Janvier, and many more.

CHAPTER XXVI.

SOME DIALECT NOVELISTS AND OTHERS.

Dialects. — English is the language of the United States, and yet, in this big country, especially in places where the railroad and the schools have not come, as up in mountain hollows or in out-of-the-way country districts, there are many people who talk a peculiar form of English, so mispronounced, so ungrammatical, that it sounds very queer to those who never heard it before. We say that they speak a "dialect." Many of our story writers, struck with the peculiar ways of people in certain localities, have written stories about them, giving their talk, their manner of thinking, etc. We call such stories "dialect stories."

Most of our novelists have come from New England, and so New England ways have been oftenest described, women having done this the best. Mrs. Stoddard, wife of the poet, wrote, before the war, three powerful novels of New England life. Sarah Orne Jewett gives us the more pleasant, quiet side, as in *Deephaven;* Mary E. Wilkins describes the middle class, and is a new writer. Elizabeth Stuart Phelps Ward, who has written *Jack* and *The Madonna of the Tubs,* short stories of the fishing villages of New England, — for she has done much among the fishermen, — writes, too, of the world beyond, telling her ideas of heaven in *The Gates Ajar* and *The Gates Between.* Her father and grandfather were clergymen, and she at thirteen published her first story in the *Youth's Companion.* Mary Hallock Foote writes of the mountains and mines of the far West, as in the *Led-Horse Claim.* Mary Hartwell Catherwood has gone back to the days of La Salle, in her *Romance of Dollard* and *The Story of Tonty;* but she and Mrs. Foote are not "dialect writers." Blanche Willis Howard's *One Summer* is as bright as her story of *Guenn* is pathetic. Constance Fenimore Woolson, another popular novelist, grandniece of Cooper, wrote *Anne, Rodman the Keeper*, and *Castle Nowhere;* also some poems, as *Kentucky Belle.*

The slavery, war, and reconstruction periods, in the South, were not prolific, but she now has a number of fine authors, many of whom are dialect writers. They have photographed the negro as he used to be, the mountains of Tennessee and of Georgia, and the old creole life of Louisiana. The most popular novelist of the war itself is John Esten Cooke, who wrote many stories, as *Surry of Eagle's Nest, Hilt to Hilt,* and *Mohun* (which bring in the Southern generals); *Leatherstocking and Silk, Virginia Comedians*, and *The Youth of Jefferson.*

George W. Cable, of Louisiana, has introduced us into a new world, the swamps near New Orleans. The quaint creole tongue, the queer negro patois, and the curious old slave songs are truthfully described. In the forests and prairie marshes of Louisiana there is a race of people descended from the exiles of Acadia and Nova Scotia, "Evangeline's people." The "Cadjiens" are silent, untaught, with the wonderfully simple ways of their Acadian ancestors. As we read of them in *Bonaventure,* we feel that their manner of life must soon pass from existence. Courage and perseverance are taught in the story of Cable's life. At fourteen he was fatherless, and, being too poor to stay at school, went into a store. While he was a soldier in the Confederate army he studied Latin, mathematics, and the Bible. Intensely religious, he gave up a position on the New Orleans *Picayune* because he was required to write notices of theaters; and so he had to go back to clerking. His sketches, *Old Creole Days*, having pleased the readers of the *Century*, he followed them by a good many novels on similar subjects, soon being able to devote himself to literature entirely. He is also a lecturer, and reads from his own works as no one else could do, for he has caught, as others have not, the intonations of the creole patois. *The Grandissimes* and *Dr. Sevier* are two of his works.

Another Southern writer who enchants his audience with readings from his own pen is Thomas Nelson Page, a Virginian, in whose veins Virginia's bluest blood flows. Born in Clay's county, Hanover, in 1853, his early education was obtained from a prayer-book and from Scott's novels as he stood at his mother's knee. We have no doubt that his *Two Little Confederates* shows us his home, Oakland, as it was during the war, and that he is one of those same little "Confeds," for a part of the army was stationed near his home for two years. His stories for grown people are nearly all of the same kind, pathetic and amusing incidents told in the dialect of the "quality nigger" of Virginia. It is an uncommon person that does not melt into tears over *Marse Chan* and *Meh Lady*, though there are smiles rippling through the stories also.

A third writer from the South has caught for the coming boys and girls a vanishing phase of existence, rescuing for them the delightful darky stories of " Brer Rabbit " and " Brer Fox "—stories which children never tire of hearing, and which only the colored mammies and uncles knew how to tell, until Joel

Chandler Harris remembered and reproduced them. Grown people, too, enjoy *Uncle Remus: his Songs and his Sayings,* and love to spend *Nights with Uncle Remus,* or *A Rainy Day with Uncle Remus.* Mr. Harris is a Georgian, who, with a boyish love for reading and but few chances for education, was fortunate enough to make the acquaintance of an old gentleman with two hobbies—one the collecting of books, the other the publishing of a newspaper in the country. He wanted a boy to learn the printer's trade. Joel Harris applied, and from that time, when he was twelve years old, he has been engaged on the press. But it was not until he became one of the editors of the Atlanta *Constitution* that he found his talent, for it was almost an accidental discovery. Being asked to furnish some negro-dialect sketches, he recalled his nights spent in the negro cabins listening to the darky folk lore, and from memory began to write these tales. To his surprise, publishers wrote to beg for more of such stories. They were copied and praised both here and in England, and some of them have been translated into French. Uncle Remus is to children as real as Mother Goose. Mr. Harris keeps on with his heavy labors as editor, but he has taken time to write *At Teague's Poteet* and *Trouble on Lost Mountain*—*not* negro stories. Perhaps *Free Joe* is his most pathetic attempt. Critics predict that he will be one of our best novelists, but no novel will give so much pleasure as the stories which Uncle Remus used to repeat to the little seven-year-old boy who slipped away so often down to the cabin. The astonishment felt by Mr. Harris at his own success reminds us of Richard Malcolm Johnston, also a Georgian.

Mr. Johnston was fifty-seven years old when Sidney Lanier's persuasions induced him to send a tale to the *Century*. His accounts of the old-fashioned, quaint " crackers " of middle Georgia amused and pleased the most refined tastes, and five books have been published by him, consisting almost entirely of short stories. *The Dukesborough Tales* will stand as his contribution to our literature.

Charles Egbert Craddock. — What Cable has done for creole life a woman has done for mountaineer life in Tennessee. This woman is Miss Mary Noailles Murfree, or "Charles Egbert Craddock," of Tennessee, near Murfreesborough. Lamed by paralysis in childhood, she thought, read, and studied all the more for her misfortune. The battle of Murfreesborough being fought where her birthplace stood, the family sought refuge in a cottage on the mountains. *Where the Battle was Fought* is a memory of that time. *The Dancin' Party at Harrison's Cove* was her first published story ; *The Prophet of the Great Smoky Mountains* her first novel ; *In the Clouds* is another, all being of similar character.

Edward Eggleston, after some self-education, became a young Methodist circuit rider in southern Indiana, a region then on the frontiers, and it is this section and period which he recalls in *The Hoosier Schoolmaster, The Hoosier Schoolboy, Roxy*, and *The End of the World*. *The Graysons* is a story in which Lincoln is introduced as a young lawyer managing his first case. For the last twelve years Dr. Eggleston has devoted all his strength to studying up our colonial times, for he is preparing a history of *Life in the Thirteen Colonies*. Some chapters have already been published in the magazines. For school children he has written a *History of the United States*.

Captain Charles King, who has had thrilling adventures among the Indians, and has lived long in the army, appeals to journals and note books, and finds material right at his hand for his stories of gar-

rison life on the frontier. Some of these stories are
for the older people, some of them for children.

Other Minor Writers. — James Lane Allen, from
Kentucky, writes of his own section. Lafcadio Hearn
gives hope of doing some first-class work, if he does
not become unreadable through the use of too much
strange dialect. E. W. Howe is original, and tells of
a class of people he knows well. H. C. Bunner (for
some time editor of *Puck*) wrote amusingly of old New
York. And the list keeps on getting longer and longer
as day by day new writers come to the front.

Summary. — NEW ENGLAND NOVELISTS : Elizabeth
B. Stoddard, *Two Men, Temple House.* Sarah
Orne Jewett, *Deephaven, Country Byways.* Mary
E. Wilkins, *Jane Field, A Humble Romance, and
Other Stories.* Elizabeth Stuart Phelps Ward,
Massachusetts; *Madonna of the Tubs*, and other
short stories of New England ; *Gates Ajar* and
Gates Between, on the future life. Mary Hal-
lock Foote, stories of mining life ; *The Led-Horse
Claim, John Bodewin's Testimony.* Mary Hart-
well Catherwood, stories of the seventeenth cen-
tury in America ; *Story of Tonty, Romance of
Dollard.* Blanche Willis Howard, Maine ; *One
Summer, Guenn.* Constance Fenimore Woolson
(1845–94), from Ohio ; *Castle Nowhere, Rodman
the Keeper, Anne.*
SOUTHERN WRITERS : John Esten Cooke (1830–86),
Virginia ; Stories of the war and many others ;
*Surry of Eagle's Nest, Hilt to Hilt, Leather-
stocking and Silk.* George W. Cable (1844–),
New Orleans ; writes of creole life ; *Madame
Delphine, Bonaventure, The Grandissimes, Dr.
Sevier.* Thomas Nelson Page (1853–), Vir-
ginia ; writes negro-dialect stories ; *Marse Chan,*

Meh Lady, In Ole Virginy. Joel Chandler Harris (1848–), Georgia; editor and story teller; *Uncle Remus: his Songs and his Sayings, Nights with Uncle Remus, A Rainy Day with Uncle Remus,* all a collection of negro folk-lore stories; *At Teague's Poteet, Free Joe.* Richard Malcolm Johnston (1822–), Georgia; *The Dukesborough Tales,* stories of Georgia "cracker" life. Mary Noailles Murfree ("Charles Egbert Craddock") (1850–); writes of the mountaineers of Tennessee; *The Prophet of the Great Smoky Mountains, In the Tennessee Mountains* (collection of stories), *In the Clouds, Down the Ravine,* for young people.

OTHER STORY WRITERS: Edward Eggleston, Indiana; *The Hoosier Schoolmaster, The Hoosier Schoolboy, Roxy, The End of the World, The Graysons,* also historian. Captain King; writes of frontier soldier life; *The Colonel's Daughter, The Deserter.* Lafcadio Hearn, *Youma, Stray Leaves from Strange Literature* (stories, legends, etc., from other languages). James Lane Allen, of Kentucky; writes Kentucky sketches. E. W. Howe, Indiana; *The Mystery of the Locks, The Moonlight Boy.* H. C. Bunner, poet and story writer, humorous; wrote of life in old New York.

Names not in Chapter: Henry Harland ("Sidney Luska"); writes of Jewish life in New York City. Alice French ("Octave Thanet"), Massachusetts; has written of trans-Mississippi life; *Expiation, Knitters in the Sun.* John Habberton, *Helen's Babies, Brereton's Bayou.* Mrs. Harriet Prescott Spofford, Maine; *The Amber Gods.*

CHAPTER XXVII.

ESSAYISTS, CRITICS, AND MISCELLANEOUS WRITERS.

Charles Dudley Warner is an observant, entertaining essayist. Born in Massachusetts in 1829, he began writing for the papers while a student at Hamilton College. He tried surveying and law, was editor of the Hartford *Courant*, traveled, and wrote letters of his travels, as *My Winter on the Nile*. His essays are humorous, meditative, and critical, full of truth, common sense, fun, and kindliness, with a longing in them to help on all worthy endeavor. *Back-log Studies* is in the meditative vein; *My Summer in a Garden* gets fun out of radishes and potatoes; *Their Pilgrimage* weaves a description of our summer resorts into a love story; *In the Wilderness* carries us camping into the Adirondacks, where black bears and deer hunts add zest to the entertainment; *Being a Boy* is a true picture of boyhood when Warner was a lad.

George William Curtis.—Warner's name suggests that of George William Curtis, the conductor of the Editor's Easy Chair in *Harper's Magazine*—a department discontinued when Curtis died in 1892, for nobody else could fill that chair as he had filled it. He knew much of men and life, having tried clerking, living at Brook Farm, farming, and traveling. From youth he was a journalist. Many of his books are collections of his magazine and newspaper articles. *Lotus Eating, Nile Notes of a Howadji*, and *The Howadji in Syria* are narratives of travel. *Prue and I*

197

consists of sketches. *Trumps* is a novel. *The Poti-phar Papers* makes fun of fashionable society. Curtis was popular as a lecturer and political orator, always working for civil-service reform. His idea was that men should vote for the best men and best measures, no matter to which party they belonged.

Donald G. Mitchell. — A third man who has traveled, lectured, and written essays is Donald G. Mitchell, or "Ik Marvel." One can hardly help liking *Reveries of a Bachelor* and *Dream Life.* Mr. Mitchell can scarcely be excelled as a writer, especially for young people. Country life, books, and children were his delight, and whatever he says on these subjects he makes delightful. *My Farm at Edgewood* and *Landscape Gardening* are books of practical value. *Fresh Gleanings* is a book of travels.

Agnes Repplier. — A charming woman writer has recently appeared, Miss Agnes Repplier, who loves children and writes for them. *Essays in Idleness,* and *Books and Men* are very pleasant reading.

"**A literary naturalist,** now and always an essayist," is the description which John Burroughs gives of himself. His subjects are taken from "all out-doors." He points out so much to be seen and heard while taking a winter's walk, or while sitting quietly on one's doorstep, that never again do we dare speak of a common stroll on wintry roads, or even of a scene in the back yard, as stupid. *Wake Robin, Winter Sun-shine,* and *Indoor Studies* represent his chosen themes. His essays on Thoreau and Emerson show another side of him. He can tell a great deal about a "chip-munk," a "musk rat," the "apple," and all kinds of everyday animals and trees. He says: "Some persons seem to have opened more eyes than others — they see with such force and distinction," and he himself is one of these people, I am sure.

Guides in Natural Science. — Another sentence in the same essay, "How many eyes did Audubon open!" reminds me that, though scientists, merely as such, cannot be given a place in such a little volume as this, there are a few guides in the study of Nature whom I must mention. They are Audubon, the ornithologist, who will point out accurately by word and picture every bird of field and forest; Gray, the botanist, who will show *How Plants Grow* and *How Plants Behave;* and Agassiz, the Swiss-American philosopher, who made natural science thrillingly alive to his pupils. Audubon died in 1851, but his books and his plates of birds will always be in season. He and his devoted wife tramped through swamp and forest together, intent on one object, that of learning more about the winged creatures of the air. When a little boy he had begun studying birds and making drawings of them, and he studied painting under a great French painter. After many years of hard work he published *Birds of America*, with a life-size colored plate of each bird. With a South Carolina friend, Dr. Bachman, he prepared *Quadrupeds of North America.* Audubon was of French blood, although a native of Louisiana, and wrote in French more naturally than in English. Agassiz is ours only by adoption, for he was born in Switzerland. He was professor at Harvard, and lived in America many years, doing more than any other man to awaken a popular interest in natural science. Longfellow was his devoted friend, and both he and Whittier wrote poems about him. Longfellow's *The Fiftieth Birthday of Agassiz* very beautifully tells of " Nature, the old nurse," taking

"the child upon her knee,
Saying, ' Here is a story book
Thy Father has written for thee.'

> " 'Come, wander with me,' she said,
>   'Into regions yet untrod,
> And read what is still unread
>   In the manuscripts of God.' "

So diligently did Agassiz devote himself to reading that "story book" of Nature that when offered large sums to lecture he answered briefly, "I have not time to make money." Asa Gray, another professor at Harvard, was a distinguished botanist who took the pains to write several volumes not too learned for the young people to understand, as his *Botany for Young People.* His *Flora of North America* tells of all our plants. As Gray understood all about plants, so Commodore Matthew Maury understood about the winds, the tides, the ocean currents. His discoveries have guided thousands of ships, and his *Physical Geography of the Sea* will guide you into a knowledge of the wonders of the deep. The Southern children know him by his schoolbooks.

Literary Specialists. — Besides specialists in science we have many in literature and literary criticism — people who make a study of literature, and who examine and review the works of others. Edwin Percy Whipple was the first who gave himself up to such work, and his criticisms are generally to be depended upon. *Literature in the Age of Elizabeth* and *Literature and Life* are rich in thought and study. Richard Grant White was our best musical critic and one of our best Shakespearean scholars, and his *Every-day English* and *Words and their Uses* are helpful in composition writing.

You will see hundreds and hundreds of useful books in the great libraries, and especially books on literary and religious subjects. But the authors of most of these books can have no place in a text-book on literature. America has had many theologians and pulpit orators of whom she is justly proud, such as Dr. Hodge, Henry Ward Beecher, Phillips Brooks, and others. Most of these, however, give place soon after they are gone to living preachers.

Summary. — ESSAYISTS: Charles Dudley Warner (1829-   ), Massachusetts; *My Summer in a Garden, Back-log Studies, Being a Boy, Their Pilgrimage.* George William Curtis (1824–92), Rhode Island, traveler and lecturer, political orator; *Nile Notes of a Howadji, The Howadji in Syria, Potiphar Papers, Prue and I, Trumps, Lotus Eating.* Donald G. Mitchell, "Ik Marvel" (1822-   ), Connecticut, lecturer, professor; *The Reveries of a Bachelor, Dream Life, My Farm at Edgewood.* John Burroughs (1837-   ), New York, literary naturalist; *Wake Robin, Winter Sunshine, Indoor Studies.*

SCIENTISTS: John J. Audubon (1780–1851), Louisiana, ornithologist; *Birds of America,* with colored plates drawn by him. Louis Agassiz (1807–73), Switzerland, scientist, professor at Harvard; *Methods of Study in Natural History, A Journey in Brazil.* Asa Gray (1810–88), New York, botanist, professor at Harvard; *How Plants Grow, How Plants Behave, Flora of North America.* Commodore Matthew Maury (1806–73), Virginia, learned in physical geography; *Physical Geography of the Seas.*

CRITICS: E. P. Whipple (1819–86), Massachusetts, lecturer and essayist; *Literature and Life, Literature of the Age of Elizabeth.* Richard Grant White (1821–85), New York, musical critic; *Life of Shakespeare, Words and their Uses.* Agnes Repplier, Pennsylvania; *Essays in Idleness, Books and Men.*

CHAPTER XXVIII.

AMERICAN HUMORISTS.

Americans love a joke supremely. It is the wit and humor sparkling through the pages of Holmes, of Lowell, and of half of our best-loved authors, that first gained for them the popular favor. Every paper, and almost every magazine, has its funny column. *Puck*, *Judge*, and *Life*, and several other periodicals, exist for the special purpose of amusing. If they sometimes accomplish serious results and promote real reforms, they do it with the powerful weapon of sarcastic wit. Of course to keep up these funny papers and paragraphs there must be an army of humorous writers. With most of these the fun consists in exaggerations, caricatures, bad spelling, and the telling of stale jokes slightly freshened up. Such writers have no place in literature. Only two or three of the professional humorists are remembered more than a year or two, or are known outside of their own locality. "Artemus Ward," our first in point of time, aroused British laughter; "Mark Twain" has aroused the laughter of the civilized world. The latter possesses the literary gift that enables him to express his comical ideas in a delightful, cultivated manner making his works worthy of preservation.

"**Artemus Ward,**" or Charles F. Browne, was a comic lecturer rather than writer. In spite of the fact that he saw everything in a ludicrous light, or in a topsy-turvy condition, there is a sadness about his own story. Consumption killed him when he was only thirty-three. During his last years, as he joked away on the platform, convulsing his audiences with laughter, he was struggling with disease, and working to support his mother as well as himself. He was born at Waterford, Maine, and being poor had to start out for himself before he had received much education. From typesetting he turned to reporting, and soon his jokes were quoted by the papers and caught up by the clowns in the circus ring. Mr. Browne, hearing others repeat his jests, concluded he might as well use them himself, and he began his peculiar career as a lecturer under the name "Artemus Ward, showman." His lectures were perfectly and purposely absurd. He would utter such seemingly casual remarks as: "Time passed on. It always does, by the way. You may possibly have noticed that time passes on. It is a kind of way time has." And then in the same mild manner he would surprise his audience by unexpected turns, as when he thus describes the Mormons: "Their religion is singular, but their wives are plural." He would indulge in the most absurd puns, as: "I have always been mixed up with art. I have an uncle who takes photographs, and I have a servant who takes anything he can set his hands on;" or, "If spring is 'some,' June is summer;" or, "Africa is famed for its roses. It has the red rose, the white rose, and neg-roes." And then he would give utterance to wise observations not entirely hidden by their seeming waggishness. His parting advice to the Prince of Wales in a supposed talk which he recounted was: "When you git to be a king, try and be as good a man as yure mother was! Be just! Be ginerous!" To some religious people who had separated from the outside world he said: "Here you air all pend up by yerselves, talkin' about the sins of a world you don't know nothin' of. Meanwhile said world continners to resolve round on her own axletree onct in every twenty-four hours, subjeck to the Constitution of the United States, and is a very pleasant place of residence." He went West lecturing, was captured by Indians, had a hand-to-hand fight with wolves; yet in *Artemus Ward, his Travels*, such slight mishaps become pure fun. London was his next goal. Here he was a grand success. This gentle, winning man, with his impossible spelling, his fresh jokes unstained by profanity or irreverence, won many warm friends. But death was then near him. *Artemus Ward, his Book*, and *Artemus Ward in London* fail to amuse us as the living man could do, and he is now only a memory.

Samuel L. Clemens, or "Mark Twain," promises to be more than a memory as long as American humor continues to be "funny." He does not play the clown's part as so many jokers do. When a mere boy he was a printer, having been apprenticed in a printing office of Missouri, his native State. While a pilot on a Mississippi steamboat he heard, over and over, the sounder call out "Mark twain," meaning that his lead had dropped two fathoms; and Clemens chose for his pen name this quaint phrase. His *Life on the Mississippi* records some of his experiences as a steamboat pilot. In 1861, when he was about twenty-five years old, he accompanied his brother, a government agent, to Nevada. At first he acted as secretary to his brother, then he became a reporter. *Roughing It* is of this period. A trip to Hawaii suggested lecturing, but a journey round the world, resulting in *Innocents Abroad*, made him famous. No other modern book has been more laughed over.

There are touches in the volume that show an eye
for the beautiful as well as for the ridiculous, and
there is much solid information. *A Tramp Abroad*
is less widely known. He and Warner wrote together
The Gilded Age, which contains the well-known character Mulberry Sellers, the visionary speculator, who
was sure every wild scheme "had millions in it."
The story has been put on the stage. *The Prince
and the Pauper* is in different vein from his other volumes. It narrates the freak of a young prince who
exchanges his robes with a beggar boy whose face
resembles his own. Nobody will believe that the exchange has been made, and you can understand what
confusion there must have been. *Tom Sawyer* is for
young people, and *Tom Sawyer Abroad* is its sequel.
Sometimes "Mark Twain" laughs *with* what is bad
and smart, and *at* what is good.

Other Humorists. — Benjamin P. Shillaber, another printer, reporter, and lecturer, amused everybody with *Mrs. Partington*, the old lady who would use
big words though she never got the right one in
the right place. "Josh Billings," or H. W. Shaw,
made many shrewd remarks, which are bright even
without the bad spelling. Robert Burdette, now a
preacher, makes the weightiest advice easier to take
because he lightens it with pleasant wit. His own idea
about the benefit of advice is: "You take a basin of
water, place your finger in it for twenty-five or thirty
seconds, take it out and look at the hole that is left:
the size of that hole represents about the impression
that advice makes on a young man's mind." "Josh
Billings" says: "All genuine humor iz truth, and that
iz what makes it so powerphull." There is much
truth and genuine humor in this handful of his saws
and definitions: "Common sense is the instinkt of
reazon;" "Suksess has no pedigree and only a short

creed ;" " There iz a hundred different kinds ov religion, but only one kind ov piety ;" " It iz better not
to know so much than to know so much that ain't
so ;" " Flattery iz like kolone-water — tew be smelt
ov, not swallowed." His reply when asked about his
peculiar mode of spelling was : " A man has as much
rite tew spel a word as it is pronounced as he has
tew pronounce it the way it ain't spelt " — a very
convenient doctrine for those who find it hard to
wrestle with English spelling.

Summary. — " Artemus Ward," or Charles Farrar
Browne (1834–67), Connecticut ; lecturer, author
of *Artemus Ward, his Book, Artemus Ward in
London.*

" Mark Twain," or Samuel L. Clemens
(1835–   ), Missouri ; *Innocents Abroad, Roughing It, A Tramp Abroad, Life on the Mississippi,
Tom Sawyer, The Prince and the Pauper, The
Gilded Age* (written in conjunction with Warner).

B. P. Shillaber (1814–90), New Hampshire ;
Life and Sayings of Mrs. Partington.

" Josh Billings," or H. W. Shaw (1818–85),
Massachusetts ; *Sayings of Josh Billings, Farmer's Almanac.*

Robert J. Burdette (1844–   ), Pennsylvania ;
known as the " Burlington *Hawkeye* Man ; "
writes humorous paragraphs for papers.

CHAPTER XXIX.

WRITERS FOR BOYS AND GIRLS.

The Children's Age. — This quarter of the nineteenth century and this country have been called " the children's age and the children's country." Of literature this is especially true. Some of our best writers — men like Hawthorne, Lanier, and " Mark Twain ;" women like Helen Hunt Jackson and Mrs. Burnett — have turned aside to write for the young folks. There was once a time when, with the exception of schoolbooks and Sabbath-school books, there was no literature at all for children. To-day the magazines for children are edited with as much care as those for older people.

One of the first men to remember the little folks was Jacob Abbott, who in his long life wrote three hundred volumes. The *Rollo Books* are for boys, the *Lucy Books* for girls, and ever so many biographies are for both. Other writers have followed his lead, and the *Zigzag Journeys*, by Hezekiah Butterworth, *The Boy Travelers*, by Colonel Knox, and the *Bodley Books*, by Scudder, are among the best books of their kind. As to history and biography, dozens of stories simplifying both can be had. C. C. Coffin's *Boys of '76* gives a lifelike account of the men and deeds of Revolutionary days. There never were such fascinating story books as now. Mary Mapes Dodge's *Hans Brinker* is so true to life that the Dutch lads

and lassies can hardly believe it was not written by
one who had skated on their canals every winter.
Donald and Dorothy is by the same writer.

Sunday-school Books. — Only a few of the books
written for the Sunday-school library deserve a place
in literature.   There is scarcely a girl, however, who
could forgive the omission of the works of Mrs. Prentiss and of Mrs. Whitney.   Mrs. Prentiss was the
daughter of the sainted minister Edward Payson,
and she - was like her father.   Her busy life as
teacher and as wife and mother absorbed most of
her time, and her books were written in a wonderfully short period.   *Little Susy's Six Birthdays*
took only ten days.   Her *Stepping Heavenward* is
loved by thousands; for what girl ever read it and
did not see in Katy, the heroine, a copy of herself !
The Little Preacher and *The Flower of the Family* are
also popular.   Mrs. A. D. T. Whitney tells of *Real
Folks.   We Girls* and *The Other Girls* are just like
the live, flesh-and-blood girls who read about them —
not too good to be natural.   *Faith Gartney's Girlhood*
is an especial favorite among Mrs. Whitney's numerous
volumes.

J. T. Trowbridge. — And now we come to two
writers whom all young people claim as their own especial favorites — J. T. Trowbridge and Louisa M.
Alcott — one being claimed by the boys, the other by
the girls.   The lives of both are as interesting as their
stories.   Trowbridge was born in a log cabin; but
the cabin was blessed with an educated mistress and
a master with brains.   The boy when he was fourteen could turn a furrow as well as any man, and
while he was turning furrows he turned rhymes in his
head.   At sixteen he had some of these verses printed,
and from that day he was bent on being a poet.
Between the times of milking cows, foddering cattle,

and shoveling paths he studied without a teacher both Latin and French. The reading and exercises he could manage, but he could pronounce only as the words were spelled. After his father's death he went to an academy a short while, and at nineteen he pluckily settled himself in an attic in New York, living on crackers and cheese — "with more crackers than cheese" — and striving to win a livelihood by his pen. He published both novels and poetry, — for he did not belong then to the children, — and he was connected with several different periodicals. It was not until he began to write for boys that he found his field. *The Vagabonds* is his best-known poem. His books may be forgotten in another generation, but he has given true pleasure to the boys of this generation.

Louisa M. Alcott. — To old-fashioned girls and little women and little men of the last generation and of this too, it would seem an impossibility that Miss Alcott's stories can ever be forgotten — and I hope they are right. Miss Alcott was born in 1833. Her father was so dreamy and unpractical that he and his family were poor, desperately poor, and Louisa was the breadwinner, knowing the bitterness of poverty for many years. As a compensation she had for her friends such men as Emerson and his circle, for their home was at Concord, and Emerson was intimate with the family, and was always regarded by Louisa with love and reverence. She began a journal when she was ten, and this journal tells her story of self-sacrifice as nothing else could. In it we see her helping with the housework, reading *Pilgrim's Progress*, Scott, and Plutarch, planning at thirteen her one purpose, "to work really to be good," writing poems, stories, and plays. These were the plays the "little women" acted, for, strange to say, the quiet maiden had a passion for the stage, and even longed to be an actress. She taught school, sewed, and, though so cultured and clever, did not disdain to go out as second girl in a family that was kin to her. She says, " I could do the wash and was glad to earn my two dollars a week."

Though her stories were accepted sometimes, there was a necessity for constant contriving, and she kept on " dishwashing, sewing, and dusting," and had some dark hours hunting employment. She served in hospitals as nurse during the war, and had typhoid fever, from which she never entirely recovered. Her *Hospital Sketches* was successful, and she wrote stories rapidly now, and was paid for them, but they were " trashy." A firm demanded a girls' book. Reluctantly she tried the writing of one, and gave an account of her own girlhood in the volume called *Little Women*. From that time her dream of making the family independent became a reality. Every debt was paid by her. Each new volume that followed meant either a trip for May or a home for her widowed sister, or something for somebody else. Yet from this time on there was constant suffering from ill health and from many sad afflictions. One sister, " Beth," had died years before ; her mother followed, then her beloved May. Up to the end she tried to work, and when no longer able to read or write she busied herself with fancy work. Her father had been stricken with paralysis in 1882, but had lingered, tended by her as long as it was possible, and only a day or so after he passed away she too laid down the burdens of life. Very slowly had the rewards of literature come to her ; not until she was thirty-five had fame and fortune begun to flow in. But to-day *An Old-fashioned Girl, Little Women, Little Men, Under the Lilacs*, and *Eight Cousins* are read and re-read by children the world over, and Miss Alcott's lessons of self-sacrifice and love of duty are taught to their young hearts. Is not that a better reward than any heights of glory she might have reached by easier paths?

Summary.—Jacob Abbott (1803–79), *Rollo Books*, *Lucy Books*, and biographies. Thomas W. Knox, *The Boy Travelers*. Hezekiah Butterworth, *Zigzag Journeys*. Horace E. Scudder, *Bodley Books*. Charles C. Coffin, *Boys of '76*. Mary Mapes Dodge, *Hans Brinker*, *Donald and Dorothy*. A. D. T. Whitney, *Real Folks*, *We Girls*, *Faith Gartney's Girlhood*. Mrs. Prentiss (1818–78), *Stepping Heavenward*, *Flower of the Family*. J. T. Trowbridge (1827–   ), *Phil and his Friends*, and many stories for boys. Louisa May Alcott (1832–88), *Little Women*, *An Old-fashioned Girl*, *Little Men*, *Under the Lilacs*.

Some other Writers for Children: Louise Chandler Moulton, *Bedtime Stories;* also a poet and a writer of stories for older people; wrote *Swallow-Flights and Other Poems*. Jane Andrews, *Seven Little Sisters, Each and All.* "Margaret Sidney," *Five Little Peppers*, *etc.* Ruth Ogden, *A Loyal Little Redcoat.* Sarah K. Bolton, *Girls who Became Famous.*

Some of the well-known novelists, poets, etc., who have written for boys and girls are: Hawthorne, Howells, Page, Harris, Mrs. Burnett, Stockton, Hale, Eggleston, Aldrich, Miss Wilkins, Mrs. Spofford, Helen Hunt Jackson, Stoddard, Lucy Larcom, Whittier, Longfellow, Lanier, Celia Thaxter, Rose Terry Cooke, Edith Thomas, Alice and Phœbe Cary, Boyesen, Miss Murfree, Agnes Repplier, "Mark Twain," and nearly all the other living authors.

CHAPTER XXX.

What have we learned about American literature? In its hundred years it has grown to vast proportions, until it would take a very large book to tell of our poets, novelists, historians, essayists, etc. Its progress has been encouraged by magazines always eager to welcome genius or talent, or even a pleasant way of "saying things." Yet after all only a few great names have gained immortal remembrance — perhaps none. Only a few will live for another century. We name Irving, Hawthorne, Emerson, Longfellow, Whittier, Holmes, Lowell, Bancroft, Motley, and Prescott. We are confident that Bryant's *Thanatopsis* and, perhaps, Poe's *Raven* will ever have a high place. And so long as people like to laugh, " Mark Twain's " *Innocents Abroad* may be remembered. Of the living novelists — Howells, James, and others — it has been often predicted that their styles will pass away ; but may we not hope that America will yet have her Scott and Dickens ? There is no lack of entertainment and instruction, of pleasant singers, of charming essayists, of acute scholarly critics. " Of making many books there is no end."

One thing we must have seen : our authors have come from all stations — from the log cabin and from the stately mansion. Some have had every advantage that the finest schools could give ; others have had no advantages and have educated themselves. Nothing can daunt or thwart intelligence and perseverance when in combination ; nothing can keep knowledge from him who reads and thinks. Of one fact we are glad and proud : back of the noble words there have been noble lives and deeds, for of only one or two authors need any apologies be offered for the conduct of their lives.

America has been as enterprising in her literature as in everything else. Every nook and corner of the world has been explored and discovered to us. Stanley, the great African explorer, brings near to us the torrid zone, while perhaps one of our half-dozen Arctic explorers brings just as near the uninhabitable regions of the North. The fishermen of New England, the creoles of Louisiana, the negroes from Virginia to Mississippi, the mountaineers of Tennessee, the " poor whites " of Georgia, the Indians of olden times and of the far West, the miners of the Rocky Mountains, the " gilded youth " of fashionable society, have been accurately pictured in story and in essay. Every phase of existence, every emotion of the heart, every passion of our nature, has been described. For information, entertainment, and amusement we need go no farther than our own American literature. Youngest among the great nations, we hope that America has yet in store the rich ripe fruit of matured thought of which her youth has given such fair promise.

INDEX OF AUTHORS.

INDEX OF SOME WELL-KNOWN WORKS IN AMERICAN LITERATURE.

I. BOOKS.

BIOGRAPHY.

CHILDREN'S BOOKS.

CRITICISM.

ESSAYS, SKETCHES, MISCELLANEOUS COLLECTIONS, ETC.

FICTION.

HISTORY.

HUMOR.

POETRY.

TRANSLATIONS.

TRAVEL AND ADVENTURE.

II. SHORT PIECES.

SINGLE POEMS.

FAMOUS SHORT STORIES.

www.ingramcontent.com/pod-product-compliance
Lightning Source LLC
Chambersburg PA
CBHW030122030726
47498CB00007B/2503